WHEN HE SAW ME

AMELIA WILDE

Cover Design: Coverlüv

Cover Photo: KDdesignphoto/Shutterstock.com

Editing: Hot Tree Editing

To Kayla, who basically gave me permission to write this book, even though she didn't know it.

And to all my readers, for sticking with me when the going gets tough.

1

EVA

THIS PARTY IS A MISTAKE.

Not on my wonderful, gorgeous friend Whitney's part, I mean. She should throw parties. She should throw parties every Thursday of her life, until she's ninety-three and causing a ruckus in her retirement community.

It's a mistake for *me*.

I know it already, and I still feel the *zing* of the hard wood of her apartment door in my knuckles.

The thing is, when you make a mistake, you should own up to it and then *get out of that situation*. You shouldn't stand there, lingering in the hallway with a fake smile plastered to your face as if you didn't throw yourself into the shower forty-five minutes ago with your heart pounding and then let the hot water blast you in the face for a solid five to clear your head.

You know. Like I did.

To be real, I knew this was a mistake way before I knocked. I knew it when I stepped onto the subway. I knew it when I stepped out of my apartment. And yes, I knew it when I stepped into the shower.

What am I *doing*?

I can still make my escape.

I turn away from the door, arranging my expression into something I hope resembles *oh shit, I forgot something very important for my Friday night plans*, and at that moment, the door swings open and Whitney, my fireball friend from back in high school, shrieks, "Eva!" She launches herself at me with such force that her hug almost takes us both to the carpet. "Sorry," she says with a laugh, releasing me in the nick of time. "I'm so glad you could make it. *So* glad. It's been way too long since we went to Vino, or anything else. Come in, come in! Everybody else is here."

"I—" I motion vaguely toward the stairwell, but

Whitney doesn't even see it. She's too busy steering me into the apartment. It's *nice*. It's bright and clean...

...and full of people.

Not *full*. There's room to walk. But there are four couples, and as nice as the place is—the countertop still has that original sheen to it—it's not huge, and my heart goes right up into my throat.

Whitney closes the door behind us. "Everybody, my famous book writer friend Eva is here!"

I feel the rift in the conversation like it's the ground dropping out from under me and swallow down the urge to throw up. Instead, I opt for a weird little wave and try not to look anyone in the face. While I simultaneously try to pretend I'm not sweating. It's real cute.

Whitney steps into the kitchen and I follow her. There's no way I can face the crowd in the living room, which looks—from the corner of my eye—like it's all couples. I recognize Summer Sullivan. The man next to her, beer in hand, is her husband Dayton. And there's Wes, Whitney's husband. They're the most opposite people I've ever seen attract in my life.

The rest of the guests are people I've never seen before. At least, I think I haven't. I'm not going to look.

I focus all my attention on Whitney, who is already having a conversation I'm not part of.

"—back to selling insurance part-time, just for the benefits. I'm sure you don't have to worry about that kind of thing, but it gives me a certain...peace of mind. A few hours three days a week isn't so bad, and it gives me time for rehearsal." Whitney opens the oven, lifts out a tray of appetizers, and breathes in deep. "These are like a fancy version of Pizza Rolls. You *have* to try one when they're a little cooler."

"Rehearsal." I latch on to the most important word Whitney spoke. "You got a new show?"

"I did." Whitney beams. "Off-Broadway, but I got the lead, and it's contemporary. A workingwoman. There's a wealth of creativity in the classics, but when it comes to reflecting the rich life experiences of—" She seems so happy, and so confident, and so *settled* in her life, as if smooth sailing is guaranteed. It's making me feel insane.

"Eva Lipton." The voice comes from just off my shoulder and I don't recognize it, which makes a muscle in the back of my neck tense. "I am *so* thrilled to meet you. I never thought—"

Well, I can't stand here staring at Whitney like a total asshole.

The woman who has approached me is petite and blonde, her hair piled on top of her head in the kind of messy bun that looks best with fine, blonde hair. I will never know such riches. She smiles up at me, almost grimacing.

"I don't want to, you know, *attack* you at Whit's party, but I—"

Don't say it. Don't say it. Don't say it.

She leans in.

"I am the *biggest* fan. I just *love* your books so much that I can't even..." Her hands go to her chest. "I can't stand it. My heart..." She closes her eyes as if it's causing her actual pain. "My heart can't take much more of a wait, if you know what I mean. I know your third book isn't supposed to publish until next year, but nine months is such a long time from now, and—"

"Eva, this is Christine." Whitney butts in, and I've never been more grateful to anyone in my life. "But I could never forgive myself if I interrupted the blooming of this beautiful friendship for even a moment." Then, with a little bow, she goes back to the plate of fancy pizza rolls and I'm left in Christine's clutches.

She's still smiling hard at me, and clearly she's moved past being sorry for attacking me at the party and is now firmly in drinking-my-blood territory. Part of me *loves* her. Part of me thinks, *You know what? I could be friends with this woman.*

But the other part of me is desperate for her to shut up.

She does not shut up.

"*The Miracle Girl* literally kept me up all night." Her hand flutters at her chest. "Like this, the whole time. My husband was pissed, but I couldn't stop reading. I ate that book alive, and then I bought a second copy because I pretty much destroyed the first one—"

Thank you. I'm so glad to hear you loved it. Fans like you mean the world to me. It's all true. It's all so true. Without people like Christine, I'd be nowhere. But the awful truth is that even *with* people like Christine, I am nowhere. All the words I should say stick in my throat. Is my throat swelling up? Please, say that my throat's not swelling up.

"—the way, Whitney didn't give you away. She only said her writer friend Eva from school was coming, and

I recognized you from a picture and then that book jacket." Christine raises both hands in the air. "Seriously, though, I *totally* respect your privacy and I would never post, like, any pictures online or anything. Not that I've taken pictures of you." She laughs nervously. "Oh, God, I'm making myself sound like a total creep. Listen, all I wanted to say was that *The Miracle Girl* is pretty much my favorite book of all time and of course my all-time favorite thriller and nobody can do it better than you."

I smile my press interview smile and reach for *I couldn't be happier that you loved The Miracle Girl,* but Christine is. Not. Done.

"I *know* you're going to outdo it with the next one, which would be unbelievable. I mean, it would really be unbelievable if you wrote a better book than *The Miracle Girl,* but I have total faith that you can do it. *And* I'm waiting with bated breath." She chuckles. "I hope that's a little bit inspiring, anyway, just knowing I'm living my day-to-day life spending every spare moment daydreaming about this new book of yours. And...if you wanted to drop any hints about what the title's going to be, I would guard that secret with my *life.*" She's so hopeful it nearly kills me. "Have I said it enough? You're the *best.*"

At this point, it would almost be better if she kept talking, but the hum of conversation from the living room does nothing to fill the silence.

It stretches out, and out, and out.

I open my mouth.

Time to say something. Time to say all the right things to this lovely woman, who is devoted to my work, who will probably buy not one but *two* copies of my book the moment it's available for preorder, who has absolutely no idea I am the book world's biggest fraud.

"I..."

Christine is breathless with anticipation. She is actually holding her breath.

"...have to go."

She's already nodding by the time she understands, and then I have to watch her face fall from excited hope to utter confusion. Her expression careens into disappointment. I can't take it anymore. I turn on my heel and go.

But I can't go to the door of the apartment. I just *got* here. I can't abandon my friend's party like an asshole —or worse, like a diva. Like I can't handle being approached by my own readers. They'd all think I was pissed, and I'm not. I'm not.

I brush past Whitney to the sliding doors leading to her tiny balcony.

"Eva?"

I don't stop for Whit. I yank open the door and step outside onto the little balcony. It smells like fresh wood, like it was built only yesterday. There's enough room for two patio chairs and the tiniest patio table I have ever seen, upon which is perched a bright bouquet that looks a little lopsided. It's *totally* Whitney. And I'd compliment her on it, but I'm too busy grabbing the railing and trying to breathe. While, of course, pretending to look out over the block below.

The sliding door *whooshes* behind me. "Girl. What's going on?"

I stand up straight and dig through my purse, not knowing what I'm looking for until my hand makes contact with a pen. "Nothing." I work that press-interview smile *hard* and whip out the pen. "An idea. Struck me. I've got to get it down before it flies right out of my head and into the ether. Nothing ever comes back from the ether."

"Eva—"

"You know how it is, when you're deep in the writing process and you have that one *idea* that's going to smooth everything out and make it sing. Okay, maybe you don't know exactly how it is, but I'm sure similar things happen during shows. When everything is gelling except that *one* guy who keeps singing off key..." I scribble a random mark onto the first available page in the notebook.

Whitney steps onto the balcony. "Eva."

"Yeah?"

"Are you okay?"

I look up into her face, and there is nothing but concern written there. She's not looking at me to be her favorite writer. This is my oldest friend. To her, I'm still Eva Lipton, no matter how many books I write.

Or don't write.

"Yeah." I try to make the word light and it hitches coming out of my mouth. I wave my hand in the air to bat it away. "I need a minute to write this down. And pull myself together a little bit. The adrenaline from the inspiration can be a little overwhelming." I put the pen to the notepad and jot...something...down.

Whitney doesn't say anything. "I...don't believe you."

"It's really—"

"I don't expect a phenomenal acting job from someone who's not a professional, but Eva, those were the least convincing sentences I've ever heard come out of your mouth. And I was there when you told me you definitely didn't have a crush on Rob McKenzie."

"I *didn't* have a crush on Rob McKenzie."

Whitney rolls her eyes. "Okay."

"I *do* have to write down this idea."

"Eva."

"A minute, Whit, I swear. One minute."

Someone calls to her from inside—Wes?—and Whit turns her head an inch, eyes still on me. "I'll be right there." Then she stabs a finger in my direction. "You can stay out here. For a minute. Then I'm coming back."

2

BENNETT

"Who's that?"

I came to the kitchen to get another beer, and life has rewarded me with the most incredible view. Auburn curls spilling over her back. A little black T-shirt that hugs her waist and slips down over her hips. Eyes wide, looking a little trapped.

In other words, my favorite thing in the world: a mystery.

I didn't expect to find one at Wes and Whitney's apartment. Wes is an Army buddy from back in the day. We have a closeness borne of getting blown up together. And then...you know, the part where I went to Afghanistan for a year and a half and found out why. That's another story, and right now it doesn't matter at all. No. What matters is this mystery woman.

"Whit, who *is* that?"

Wes's wife, Whitney, with her usual mess of dark hair and a black dress with a huge floral pattern that would look ridiculous on anyone else, looks at me while she shuts the door. She's scowling. "My friend Eva."

"What's she doing on the balcony?"

The scowl turns to something more quizzical. "I see that look on your face, Ben. Don't do it. Don't get into it like this. I don't know what's going on with her."

"I'm not getting into anything." I crane my neck to look around Whitney, at that fall of auburn, the slope of her shoulders. "Why is she out there, though?"

"I don't know."

"I'm going to find out."

"Ben—"

"I just want to know why she's on the balcony by herself in the middle of your party."

Whitney sighs. "You know that's never how it happens."

"A simple conversation?"

"No conversation with you is ever simple. And really, what *is* a simple conversation?" She cocks her head and looks at me through narrow eyes. "Is it the content, or only the emotional landscape upon which—"

"Nice try. Let me through."

Whitney opens her arms wide, blocking my path. "Don't do it. She's not one of your projects." The light from outside beams in around her like she's an avenging angel. And she can be an avenging angel, according to Wes. Whitney really is a force of nature.

But Eva, standing outside, is a law unto herself. A law of physics. Like gravity. Nobody blames a rock for falling to the earth. I can't even blame myself for trying to be at her side. It makes no sense, but I don't have the luxury of an apple tree to sit beneath until understanding strikes.

And anyway, the only way to be inspired by anything is to get the facts. All of them. Especially the ones people don't want you to have.

"Whit. I'm going to go talk to her. It's the right thing to do. As a human."

She gives me one more long look then drops her hands

to her sides. "Well...I've done my part. I have tried my hardest, yet I am screaming into a void and the only echo—"

"Whit. It's just a conversation."

"Sure it is."

Wes comes into the kitchen then, opening the fridge himself for another beer. "Is Powell giving you a hard time? I'll punch him if he is."

"Not me." Whitney moves past me and slinks her arm around Wes's waist. "He's going after Eva."

Wes considers this. "She could use a good—"

Whit slaps him. "Oh my God. You are filthy. She is going through *something*. I don't know *what*, and you're in here making jokes about—"

"Conversation," Wes finishes, a lopsided grin on his face. He dips Whitney back and kisses her until they're both laughing. It hurts to see it. Not that I'll ever admit that to either of them. For a moment, I consider getting to the bottom of that feeling, but...no. Out on the balcony, there's a woman who's far more arresting than my sorry soul could ever be.

I leave them in the kitchen, Whitney pulling Wes over

to the stove to show him her latest batch of appetizers, and open the sliding door.

"I'M ALMOST DONE, Whit. I'll be right in. Save me a plate."

I shut the door behind me, closing us off from the ebb and flow of the chatter inside. I didn't realize that Wes and Whitney had air conditioning until I stepped out into the early evening heat of the balcony. We're going to be heading into July in a couple of weeks, and the summer has already baked itself into the wood. "Save you a plate of what?"

Eva turns with a start. "You're not Whit."

"Very astute observation. I'm Bennett Powell."

"The shrapnel guy." Yes. I am the man who was in the Humvee with Wes and Dayton when Wes drove it over an IED. And yes, I am the one who spent almost two years of my life finding out why that IED got there in the first place. Apparently, word has gotten around. To Eva, at least. She doesn't wait for me to answer before she gives a sharp little sigh and turns back toward the railing. Eva looks so melancholy, with her forearms on the wooden railing, and so much like a magazine model that I wish I had a camera. I'd tell her how fucking delicious her jean shorts look around the curve of her ass, but now's not the time.

"So you've heard the story."

"I heard the highlights. From Whit. When she and Wes were...you know, when they were finally together."

I take my beer over to the railing and look down at the street with her. She's staring down at the cars moving slowly down the block. Someone's grilling out, but I can't see where—maybe the roof, or another balcony that's hidden from view.

Beneath us, a read car pulls up to the curb and a man in a suit gets out. On the corner, a group of three teenagers are up to something furtive, but they don't have the sense to go somewhere that's actually out of view of the general public, so who knows what it is. A woman walks quickly toward the corner and out of sight, her shoulders heaving like she's crying. On the other side of the street, a guy is sitting outside of a café, elbow braced against his knees, the sitting version of what Eva's doing right now. Which one of them is she watching? I steal a glance at her out of the corner of my eye, but her gaze is far away.

So...none of them. She's just staring down at the street like a melancholy supermodel.

"What are you almost done with?"

"Hmm?" She doesn't look at me.

"You said you were almost done with something." I take a drink of my beer. "What are you doing?"

"Smoking a cigarette," she says flatly.

"Ha."

She shifts, her hips swaying from side to side, and I feel her eyes land on my face. Eva must see something there that changes her mind about talking to me. "I came out here to write down an idea I have."

"With your imaginary pen?"

"Do you always ask this many questions?" She turns to face me now, eyes narrowed. It doesn't matter that she's giving me that *look*; her eyes are a startling green. The early stages of sunset look good on her.

"Usually more."

"I'm not in the mood."

"What *are* you in the mood for?"

"Thinking." She lifts her chin and folds her arms over her chest. "About what I'm going to write."

"Does your boss pay you to skip out on parties for solo brainstorming sessions?"

A little grin, a little blush, and Eva's eyes slide to the side. I can see her pulse fluttering at the side of her neck. It's a dead giveaway.

And there's more to read in her body language. She's not enjoying the party, for one thing. Her shoulders are so tense they're almost touching her ears.

"No." She goes back for the railing and grips it with both hands. "They don't pay me for that. Only...for the finished product." Whitney never said what kind of writer she was. Maybe it's one of those blogging jobs where you have to write fifty articles a week for five cents. The set of her shoulders indicates it might not be entirely pleasant for her.

"Harsh. You should agitate for better working conditions."

Eva barks out a laugh and looks down at the corner, in the general direction of the teens. "They have no idea, do they?"

"No idea about what?"

"How simple everything is. How complicated things can get. You know. Generally. Not for me specifically."

Sure. I believe *that*.

For a flash, I wonder if she and Whitney planned this somehow specifically to reel me in. Whitney of all people knows how I am. She knows I always follow the pull of a good secret.

Eva is trembling. Whatever is on her mind is *seriously* bothering her. No, it's not her body; it's her hands. Even though she's holding onto the railing for dear life, there's still a little shake. The curiosity that was a lit match before roars into wildfire. It turns me on almost as much as the particular way her hair falls down her back does. Don't get me started on her lips, or the little pout she's wearing right now.

I put my hand on top of one of hers.

And I'll be damned, but Eva doesn't pull away.

She doesn't flinch.

She doesn't tense.

No—she *relaxes*. A little sigh escapes her lips and her shoulders move down, away from her ears.

New fact acquired: Eva likes to be touched. By me.

"What are you doing out here, Bennett Powell?" Eva's eyes are firmly down at the street, but she doesn't make even the slightest move to pull herself away. It's nothing, the way I'm touching her, palm flat against the back of her hand, fingers resting gently on hers, but the space between us heats up. It heats up more than skin has any right to, really, even in the warmth of the evening. The sensation settles over me like a blanket. A thick, heavy blanket that also has the effect of turning me on, more than the sight of her standing here did. And I don't just mean in a raunchy, sexual way, although that's true, too. In an *intellectual* way. Intellectually, I'm obsessed with the secrets she's undoubtedly keeping.

"I wanted to write down an idea I thought of."

It makes her grin, and I feel like a man who has wedged his foot in the door of a vault just in time to stop it from locking forever. "You don't have a pen."

"I can borrow one from you. You're the writer."

"Yeah." *Now* she tenses...then lets the tension go. I *have* to know more about this woman. She fled to this balcony after three minutes at a party and she's consciously trying to keep her cool. A hundred questions are on the tip of my tongue, but instead, Eva stands tall and takes in a deep breath. It reminds me of a diver preparing to plummet into the depths. "We should go back in."

"I disagree."

"You...disagree?"

With my free hand, I lift my beer off the railing and drain the rest of it. There. My obligation to this party, tenuous as it was, is now resolved. "I heartily disagree."

Eva turns to look at me, but not so far that she has to take her hand away from mine to do it. "What else did you have in mind, aside from attending the party we're both supposed to be at right now? With our *friends*?" She emphasizes the last word and the guilt is clear in her voice.

I look down at the street again, out of habit as much as anything else. The teens have moved themselves closer to the nearest building to stand in its shadow, but they're still plainly visible. The man in the suit gets back into the red car and it pulls away, into the traffic. The other man—the one outside the cafe—leans back in his seat, staring up into the sky.

There's nothing down there that could hold a candle to

her. And I'd venture to guess that nothing down there —not the teens, or the man who *clearly* has his own story in progress—holds a candle to whatever it is that made her come out here so fast. Despite her own guilt over leaving her friend.

Maybe I'm overconfident, but the next time her gaze glides over mine, I pop the question.

"Do you want to get out of here?"

3

EVA

It has to be something about his eyes. Yes. Or the body beneath the gray T-shirt. The way it clings to him suggests a man who's kept himself in shape. Maybe very good shape. Or maybe it's the very fact of the party—my loyal fan, Christine, waiting inside, all the couples—but I say yes to Ben Powell. Yes, I want to get out of here.

We get out of there.

Down on the sidewalk, I think, *Escape*. But my brain still feels clouded with worry, so I don't escape, nor do I come up with some fantastic excuse for why I really can't hang out with him at all.

Plus, he doesn't give me any time.

The moment the building's front door closes behind us, Ben says, "This way."

This way. He knows exactly where he's going. I have no idea where I'm going, with my book or with my life in this moment, but at least Bennett Powell is a confident man.

I fall in step beside him. For once, it's nice to let someone else lead, and he's honestly leading me through a strikingly gorgeous New York City evening. As we walk, the sun careens toward the skyline and the sidewalk falls into shadow. Ugh. It's so nice. My eyes are immediately grateful. It reminds me of the moment after a person turns out the light but before you start to have sex with him. Not that I've found any men in New York who want to have sex with me. Not that I've been looking.

Now's not the time to think about this.

Ben walks me around the corner, one block over and two blocks up, and by the time he stops in front of a little restaurant with a dark wood facade, the sun is setting. If I could see it, it would probably be a brilliant blaze of color, but next to these buildings, all I get is the warm afterglow.

It looks quite lovely on Ben's skin.

He pulls open the door and turns back to me with a smile. "After you."

It's an Italian place. Tiny. Maybe fifteen tables. On a Thursday night, half of them are full, and waiters in black slacks and shirts with white aprons move efficiently between the islands of linen tablecloths.

I love it instantly. It's not so silent that you just *know* it's a shitty restaurant, but it's not so crowded that someone might recognize me. There are only ambient clinks of silverware against dishes and the low hum of conversation. Nobody here is freaking out—or if they are, they're doing it very, very quietly.

"What do you think?" Ben's voice is equally calm. We're still standing far enough away from the host's station that it won't be awkward if we pretend to have an appointment somewhere else.

"How did you find this place?" I've visited Whitney's apartment twenty times, and she's never mentioned it. Not that it's particularly odd in Manhattan to not realize what riches are practically in your back yard.

"I do a lot of looking." I can feel those brown eyes on my face, but in this moment, I don't hate it. "Are you hungry?"

"I wasn't. Until just now."

It's true. I was not. I spent most of the afternoon in a state of panic and then a state of get-me-the-hell-out-of-this-party. And now I'm ravenous.

We get a table toward the back and sit in a surprisingly comfortable silence. I order my favorite thing at Italian restaurants: grilled chicken on a bed of buttered noodles. Ben orders shrimp scampi. The waitress, a blonde woman with a seriously perfect smile, validates my choice of wine, takes our menus, and leaves us with a basket of bread so soft that the first bite melts in my mouth. I'm not done eating it when Ben leans back in his seat and looks at me. There it is: that bare-skin feeling, as if my clothes are imaginary.

"Eva." My name curls from his lips like a whisper of smoke. "What's really going on?"

My shoulders tense at the question, and the little door in front of my vulnerable writer heart slams shut. I take another bite of bread, chew, swallow.

"Nothing."

He quirks an eyebrow at me, and my cheeks heat up.

"I shouldn't have tried to go to a party," I admit.

"Why not?"

"I wasn't in the mood." I think of the hour beforehand I spent pacing around my apartment trying to shake off the building anxiety. "It was a mistake."

"It might have been a mistake in the first place, but it turned into this dinner." Ben smiles and I'll be damned if it's not the sexiest thing I've ever seen. "That doesn't seem like a mistake."

On some level, it's true. The restaurant is probably the most relaxing place I've been in several months, and my editor has insisted on eating in some pretty high-end places around the city. That's mostly so she can run into other people she knows and show me off. Or maybe she's showing herself off. I can never tell. Nobody here, at least, is going to ask me who I am, and nobody is going to ask me about the book.

Ben is still watching me, in a casual sort of way, the way you might watch a piece of art. "Do you always stare at everything like this?" I ask.

"Only the things I'm interested in."

Smooth. He's so smooth.

"Well, what you see is what you get."

He laughs out loud. "I don't believe that for a second. Whitney's your best friend, isn't she?"

"I've known her a long time. I'd consider us pretty close." I don't know where he's going with this. With Whitney, it's absolutely true. Her emotions—and everybody else's—are always written plainly on her face.

"But you still didn't tell her what's making you so stressed."

"How would you know that?" I put another piece of bread on my plate and tear it in two. It's just so good.

"I saw her face after she came in from the balcony. Sort of a little frown, like...." Ben does an exact imitation of Whitney and gets it so dead on that I start to laugh and choke on the bread a little bit. He leans forward, watching me until I've taken a drink and cleared my airway, and then gracefully ignores it.

"So you can read minds, then?" My eyes are watering a little bit and I dab them with the corner of my cloth napkin.

"Yes. And I can tell you're hiding something."

The waitress, God and all of his angels bless her, comes back with the wine. I don't really care what goes with dinner. All I care about is that it's so sweet I can't taste the alcohol.

This moscato delivers.

The first sip is pure joy against my tongue, and so is the second, and by the time the waitress is back at the kitchen doors, my glass is gone.

Oh, that's *so* much better.

"I should have had some wine at Whitney's." I stare longingly at my empty glass, willing it to refill before my eyes.

Ben doesn't have a drink, and I stifle the urge to ask him why he didn't order a matching glass of wine, but the question seems too intimate somehow. Even though he's the one who whisked me to this secret hideaway of a restaurant.

Our waitress reappears and I signal her with my eyes that I need more wine. She knows instantly what I'm thinking and goes back into the kitchen, coming out with a fresh glass a moment later. I curl my hand around it and sip more slowly this time.

"What were we talking about?"

Christ, he is *attractive.* I mean, there's not an ounce of

fat on Ben's entire body, and his hair is—well, it's not so long that I wouldn't be into it, but it's not buzzed off either. I want to run my hands through it.

"You were about to tell me what you were hiding."

At this very moment, a hiccup bubbles up from my chest that I can't hide.

Ben's shoulders shake with silent laughter.

"Are you—" Another hiccup. "—*laughing* at me?"

"No." His expression goes instantly serious. "I think the bigger question is, are you drunk on one glass of wine?"

"Of course not." I take a long sip from the second glass. "Not even."

I'm not. The wine is going through me with a familiar warmth, but honestly I can't tell if it's the alcohol or Ben's eyes. Both of them are having...an effect.

"You're a bad liar. You should just give up your secret. It would be easier on us both."

"You want to know what my secret is?" The gates around my heart are slowly creaking open under the onslaught of wine. Soon I'm going to need a third glass. "You really want to know?"

Ben leans in. "Eva, I desperately want to know your secret. Why else do you think I spirited you away from that party so we could have a solo date in an Italian restaurant?"

"A solo *date*?" I squeak. "This isn't.... We're not—"

"Dinner," he says quickly. "A solo dinner. Have some more wine. You'll feel better. Oh, and tell me what you're hiding."

"I'm totally *not* hiding anything."

"Do your hands always shake when you have a secret?" This way, then that. This conversation is an ambush. I thought I was avoiding an ambush by coming with Ben, but instead I've walked right into it.

And I can't say I hate it.

I look down at the glass of wine in my hand. "They're not shaking."

"They were. Out on the balcony."

"Why are you so obsessed with the balcony?" My glass is empty, and our heaven-sent waitress is at my side immediately with a third glass.

A half-smile plays at the corner of Ben's mouth and I'm seized with the urge to kiss it right off of him. He leans toward me, flicking his eyes out to the other tables and back to my face. "Picture this. The most gorgeous girl you've ever seen enters the party you're at." If I thought my face was red before, it has to be spontaneously combusting now. "She leans away from her best friend and then...suddenly...flees to the balcony." He sits up straight again, eyes alight. "If you ask me, that's a mystery."

"And you like to solve mysteries?"

"I like to get the facts." Ben lifts his fork from next to his plate and twirls it in his fingers.

Two and a half glasses of wine on a mostly empty stomach. "What if I don't want to give you the facts?"

He leans in again, about to deliver some deep secret. "What if you *do*?"

The wine has warmed my body from my belly up to my shoulders. I feel like I'm holding a giant balloon, too large for a human to keep pinned to earth, and my only option is to...let it go.

If I just *told* Ben, maybe I'd feel freer. What's the harm, really? He doesn't know who I am, and it might be nice to spill my guts a little in a way that's not...you know, career-ending.

I don't have to tell him everything.

I'm *not* going to tell him everything.

The words gather on the tip of my tongue like a heavy thundercloud. There's no reason *not* to tell him. I've had enough wine. I've escaped enough parties. It's time. It's time to make someone else share this burden with me.

Now it's my turn to lean in. "I went out to the balcony, because I'm on a tight deadline and I'm not sure I'm going to meet it." I hear my own voice rising with worry, but it's tamped down by the wine.

"Tell me about it," he says. "I'm listening."

4

I'M NOT a big wine drinker, but if last night was any indication, you can get yourself good and drunk on it if you drink it fast enough and order a second bottle.

Which is exactly what Eva did.

Which is how she ended up in my apartment after our *lengthy* dinner ended.

And to be clear, I didn't mind it. The hiccups were cute as hell and so was she, swaying like she was wearing heels when in fact she was wearing those flat shoes that have nothing to do with dancing. I'd been torn about it, you know. I'd rather die in a nuclear blast than take advantage of her, but it didn't seem right to put her in a cab alone. It didn't even seem right to drop her off at her door. So when she leaned her head against my shoulder in the back of a surprisingly clean yellow cab and said, "I don't think I should go home..."

I didn't argue is what I'm saying.

I took that gorgeous mystery of a woman back to my apartment, supplied her with a T-shirt that looked unbelievably oversized and painfully sexy, but because I am a man of fucking honor, I only crawled in beside her and listened to her breathing even out.

Eva Lipton sleeps curled on her side, her red hair spilling over the pillow behind her. It was wild watching the last of the day's tension leave her muscles. I haven't seen anyone relax that fast in my bed for a long, long time. I praised the past version of myself for not buying a shitty mattress when I had the chance, because it was perfect for her. She hadn't really moved when I got up an hour ago and came out to the living room to work.

I have two jobs.

One job is the one that pays me. My natural obsession with getting the facts made becoming a fact-checker after I left the Army a no-brainer. It's a lot of sifting through the deep corners of the Internet and confirming details that seem insignificant until they're not. The company I work for publishes information on all kinds of content—they contract with groups in the public and private sectors—and more than once they've saved those groups from embarrassing mistakes or, worse, lawsuits. They pay me well and I can work from anywhere with an Internet connection, which means I can work on my second and more important job: getting to the bottom of how I got there in the first place.

To the Army.

And it all comes back to my father, only no matter how much of my time I devote to it, I can't make sense of the man's tangled webs. Tangled is probably an understatement. His life was full of crossed wires and strange mistakes for a man like him. He was too smart for what happened. But everything starts with him, because—

There's a rustling from the bedroom that might as well be a bullhorn in the early morning hush of my apartment. Without thinking of it, I've been listening to this sound since the moment I came out to the living room and sank into my worn-in armchair. I've been working through the latest project, but most of my attention was really on the dim haze of the bedroom, waiting, waiting....

The sun has barely risen, and I've learned another

thing about Eva Lipton: even when she's waking up in someone else's bed, she is still graceful. Quiet as a mouse, actually, which makes me curious about...how she is at other times.

My one-bedroom apartment has, through some inexplicable miracle, two bathrooms, one in the entry hall and one attached to the bedroom. I'm sure Eva's appreciating that right now. She must have gone in there, because I hear water running. Then more rustling. Getting dressed?

She pads out into view in bare feet, her flats dangling from her fingertips and her other hand clutching the handle of her purse. Sneaking. She's going to tiptoe to the door and sprint if she can get away with it.

Well.

"Hey."

Eva startles and claps her hand over her mouth to hide her sharp breath. "Christ. You scared me."

I can't help smiling at the sight of her. It's a compulsion, but I try to keep it to a minimum. "Where did you think I was?"

She bites her lips. "I don't know. Getting coffee, hopefully."

"And you were hoping to be gone before I got back."

"Yes, and..." Her voice trails off.

"What else were you hoping?"

Eva turns her face toward the enormous picture window, the light making her cheeks a deeper shade of pink. She looks deliciously rumpled like this. From sleeping in my bed. My heart pounds at the memory of it and it *just* ended. "I was hoping I could sneak out of this...mortifying situation without seeing you."

I thread my hands behind my head. "Nothing mortifying happened last night."

"Not for you."

"It's a little embarrassing to have to be such a gentleman."

"Oh, please." She scoffs. "You *loved* being a gentleman."

"I promise you, Eva, I had a *very* love-hate relationship with being a gentleman. Right now, it's trending heavily toward hate."

Eva's blush deepens and I want more than anything to take her back into that bedroom in the light of day and *really* see her. Stripped. Naked. Pink and perfect and exposed. She'd have no secrets then, and in this moment I don't care if it makes me dishonorable; I want it like I wanted water when we were in that fucking Humvee out in the desert. I want *her*.

For a moment I think she might part those lips and flirt back, but something in her face shifts and changes. It's the worst when you can see a moment slipping through your fingers. It's almost as bad as when a moment you've dreaded actually comes, exploding up through the ground, all hellfire and destruction and you're thinking, *Why, why? What's the point of all this?* But it's way too late for your Humvee, not to mention the two of your buddies up in the front.

"Stay." I let the suggestion fall softly between us, standing up at the same time and stretching out my legs. "It's still early. You haven't missed anything yet."

She didn't stay.

And yes, it was one of the greater disappointments of my lifetime. Once, when I was seven, my parents took me to the elementary school game night. There was a drawing for prizes, and one of those prizes was a detective kit. I wanted that thing more than I'd ever wanted anything, and I'd busted ass all night tearing up the games for tickets. You already know what happened at the end of the night. I didn't win the detective kit. In fact, this asshole named Peter Kulls won it and he gloated over it all the way out to his family's Jeep.

What happened with Eva hurt worse than that, though I'm still not sure why. I've known her all of thirty seconds. I let her sleep in my bed out of the sheer goodness of my heart and not any other motive whatsoever.

Eva turned her face away from the light, lips slightly parted, and I swore I could see her getting ready to agree. I didn't care if she wanted to go to bed or preferred to perch herself on my sofa, as long as she stayed. But instead, she pinned those lips together, this *look* coming into her eyes, a cross between shame and distrust that just about killed me.

"I have to go." Her voice bounced off the wall behind me, an echo like a ripple in water.

I stood where I was. "I'm not stopping you."

Then I doubled down on all of it. It was five steps to the door. Flipped the lock. Pulled it open. The air from the hallway shifted in our direction, and as she went by me, it lifted stray locks of her hair.

I let her walk away.

She didn't look back.

"What are you moping about?"

The voice that interrupts my thoughts belongs to one Ash Montgomery, who deployed for the first time three months after we did. He never talks about any women, but he has the kind of face that must attract them like moths to a streetlight. He's also tall, a little taller than I am. Occasionally, he's funny, and he's usually reliable, and sometimes pays for rounds of everyone's drink. A decent guy, if a little cagey.

He's come up beside me by the window.

"Since when does looking at this beautiful view count as moping?"

Ash laughs out loud. "You're right. It's stunning down there."

Mack's Bar is not in the finest neighborhood ever to grace the earth, and down there in the pool of light from a street lamp, a couple is fighting, jabbing fingers at one another. I take another swig of my beer.

"Tell me you're not still thinking about that IED."

I shoot him a look that says *you're being fucking stupid.*
"No, man, I'm done with all that."

"What's the faraway look for, then?"

Ash has been going to this veterans support group since it
started six months ago, around the time I moved back to the
city. He thought it was bullshit at first, but he's moved on to
asking questions, which I can appreciate, being...who I am.
It helps that we rent out the top floor of a bar in Brooklyn
for the meetings. That means there's easy access to beer,
and it's pretty casual. Sometimes, we end up playing cards,
and most nights nobody talks about being in the service.
Still, it's a good feeling to be around these guys every other
Saturday from eight o'clock onward.

Ash clears his throat and tries again. "You got somebody on your mind, or are you just being cagey to fuck
with me?"

"I'm not fucking with you." I wasn't, though I want to
ask Ash the same question. He missed four meetings in
a row then came back with a frown on his face and a
rigid way to his posture that made me think his chest
hurt. My natural instinct is to press him until I know
what happened, but that's usually not a good strategy
at a fucking support group. And I'm never going to

know what happened to him if I'm not honest. "It's somebody. Somebody who stayed the night last night."

This perks Ash right up, his blue eyes going wide. "What kind of somebody?"

"She's—" Hundreds of words bubble up to the tip of my tongue and I swallow them all down with another draw of my beer. Eva was so embarrassed this morning that she couldn't bring herself to look at me on the way out. How can I tell *any* of this to Ash? I can't sell her mortification out like that. It would be different if she were my wife, maybe, but...maybe not. "She's somebody," I settle on.

Ash makes a disgusted noise in the back of his throat and shakes his head. "Cryptic. You're such a dick. Why else are we here, if we're not going to talk?"

"Oh, you want to talk? Where were you the last— Hang on."

My phone is the thing that cuts me off. I dig it out of my pocket to see what it is, conscious of Ash watching.

"Wow," Ash says, faux disappointment ringing in his voice. "The fact that you'd interrupt our therapeutic conversation to answer a text message is hardly *supportive* of you, Ben—"

"Shut your damn mouth. Nobody texts me while I'm at these things."

He raises his eyebrows. "Oh, so it must be more important than the person standing in front of you right now."

"Undoubtedly."

"Asshole." He laughs. "You coming to the thing next weekend?"

"I'm good." I swipe at the screen to reveal the text message.

And I'll be damned.

It's from Eva.

5

EVA

IT WAS ALL A HUGE MISTAKE. Going to the party in the first place. Leaving it for dinner with Ben. Somehow—and I don't remember exactly how, but I have a hazy memory of saying something ridiculous and thinking he'd just drop me off at home—staying over at Ben's.

But the biggest error I've made in this entire situation was coming back to my own apartment.

The damn thing feels like it's closing in. It felt smaller from the moment I stepped inside. Wrong, even though I've spent most of my time the last few weeks fussing over every detail. I hate the throw pillows I got last week, and they seemed so *funny* at the time. One says *sit your ass down;* it has a line drawing of a donkey.

And the other says *you are what you eat, so I am pizza.* I have no fucking idea. They seemed right at the time, and now they seem like something I should have had in my college dorm. And I would have, only I agonized over every penny back then. Needlessly. But there's no point in beating myself up over decisions I made in college. Or the throw pillows, really, though I do hate them now. I turn them so they're both facing in.

I pace through my little collection of rooms, irritated with myself for being liked this. I have a nice apartment. The book deals were big enough that I finally got myself a place with ceilings that didn't brush the top of my head when I walked through the living room. It has big, floor-to-ceiling windows looking out over Bryant Park, and I did the whole thing in a shade of white that makes me think of flannel sheets.

I'm supposed to be happy.

And now, in my flannel sheet apartment, all I can think about is Ben Powell's eyes. To describe them as "brown" would be such a cop-out. They *are* brown, but they're multifaceted in a way that I've only ever seen in green eyes, or blue. Somehow, his eyes have flecks of...gold. Yes. It must be gold, and streaks of amber. Unlike anything else I've ever seen.

I want to see them again.

So now, hands trembling, I send a text.

Eva: I made a mistake.

I send it, and then I pace furiously back through my apartment again, swallowing down my nerves and a fresh wave of embarrassment. Could I *be* any more cryptic and ridiculous? I'm already steeped in enough mystery, being a writer, and people get sick of that shit. As they should. I should have just told him what I want. I should have just stayed over in the first place. His voice was calming, and now my apartment is a blank white echo chamber that I hate with the burning passion of a thousand suns. I have already tried music, which grated against my ears, but now the quiet is too loud. And...there's the text I've sent.

I'm about to turn my phone off and pretend I didn't do it when his answer pops up on my screen.

Ben: Was it sending this text?

Eva: Ha

I actually do laugh, a short, sharp thing.

Eva: Maybe

Ben: You know, it would be easier to open the kimono

Eva: I'm not wearing a kimono

Ben: What *are* you wearing?

I look out over Bryant Park, at all those happy, carefree people strolling across the grass, and tap out my reply.

Eva: Even if I were wearing a kimono, I wouldn't open it

Ben: What about just...telling me with words?

Eva: I'm using plenty of words right now, don't you think?

Ben: Tell me what you want, Eva. He follows this up with a gif of a man with his hand by his ear, an exaggerated *I'm listening.*

Eva: I don't know what I want. I don't even know why I'm texting you

Ben: It's because you miss me. Obviously...

I take a deep breath. I've already come this far, so

there's no sense in hauling myself back out of the water now.

Eva: I miss last night.

Ben: Coy

Eva: I'm not being coy, I'm being…

I'm losing it, is what's happening. Twin desires rage at the pit of my gut. On the one hand, I want to shut this down and pretend this isn't happening, but it *is* happening. And on the other hand…I need him. And not in some pathetic *"I need your calming presence nearby"* way, though that is true, but in the way that my body aches to be next to his. And not just for his presence. I've never felt *this* obsessed with a man's body before.

Plus, there's nobody else I can call. I'm not going to call happy, perfect Whitney, and there's nobody else. No parents. No sister. Because of me.

That's not what I want to talk to Ben about, though. Not Ben, and not anyone else.

I thought I wanted to be alone, but I do not, not with the blank page on my computer screen taunting me.

The blank text message screen on my phone taunts me

in the same way. No matter what I do, someone is always waiting for me to say something. This time, it's Ben.

I was vague with him last night at the restaurant.

I swallow the last of my pride.

Eva: Can you come over?

THE BUZZER RINGS on my intercom an hour later, and even though I'm expecting it, it makes me jump. I swear, I can feel each individual vein in my body, the blood rushing through it, getting warm, getting hot.

I push the button. "Hello?"

"It's me," he says.

I buzz him in.

The wait for him to ride the elevator up to my floor is almost as bad as the entire preceding hour. Once I knew he was coming, I sprinted for the shower. Normally, I set aside an evening to wash my hair because it's so curly, but not this time. I did my Under Extreme Pressure wash and dry, determined it mostly a success, and spent the rest of the time choosing an outfit. I want to correct the impression I gave him last night—of some lush who drank herself into sleeping over—but not overcorrect. So I don't go with a skirt suit. I go with a dress—an A-line I got from ModCloth that, upon closer examination, has books printed on it. Maybe, if I can fake it, he won't see what's really going on.

I wait in the middle of the living room, not right next to the door, so when he knocks I can casually walk across and call "coming."

My heart thuds—*one, two*—against my ribcage.

I open the door and as soon as I do, Ben is moving past me into the apartment.

"What have you already tried?" He reaches for something in his pocket. "For the writer's block?"

I shut the door and flip the deadbolt all while staring after him. "How did you know I have writer's block?"

"I had a conversation—" Ben stops, does a double take. "Were you going somewhere?"

The dress—of course, the dress. It's ten o'clock. Ben's eyes rake over it, and I see his approval on his face.

"No. Not really. I didn't have any plans."

He nods. "You look beautiful." Before I can answer, he goes on. "Whitney told me you were a writer."

I cover my face with my hands. "Oh, God. Whitney can't keep her mouth shut about anything, and now you probably know—"

"I know you're a writer. Plus, we covered that at dinner."

"We did?"

He's got his phone out, scrolling through something, but he looks up and quirks an eyebrow at me. "Yes. You told me you had a writing deadline, and then you clammed up and wouldn't say anymore."

"Well," I say primly. "There's not much more to say."

It's automatic. The dismissal. The downplay. But the instant the words are out of my mouth, Ben goes still. "I don't believe that for a second. I think you have a *lot* more to say. Otherwise, I wouldn't be here."

My face is painfully red. "What if it's just for your calming presence?"

"You seemed pretty anxious to get away from my calming presence this morning."

"Obviously that was a mistake."

"Yeah," says Ben, and I want to know what it would be like to kiss him. He has nice-looking lips. Honestly, he could be a model on the cover of a romance novel. Looking at him, I'm sure I could write one. "If you, as a writer, need me that much, I assumed it would be because of writer's block."

"Whitney didn't...tell you anything more than that?"

"All she told me was that you are her oldest friend, you are a writer, and you were coming to the party."

"Right. And you're not an idiot, so you figured it out."

"Writer, deadlines—all the clues pointed in the same direction. What else could it be?"

I want to say *"I'm terrified."*

But I don't.

Instead I let out a big breath that I've been holding.

"Okay. Yes. It's a deadline. It's—it's a hard deadline, and I'm not going to make it."

"There are tons of things we can try." *We can try* hits my ears like three pebbles hitting the surface of a still lake. "Going for a walk. A dinner out. Though—we did that last night, and we both know how that turned out." His eyes move back to mine and a flush moves over every inch of my skin. It's so dangerous to have him see me like this.

Ben glances back down at the phone and his eyes darken with what looks like anticipation, even though we didn't come anywhere close— "Centering activities."

"What's a centering activity? Do tell."

"Massages. Sex." Those eyes flick back up to mine, and you know what? I could go for that. I could go for a quick, hot fuck. I could go for Ben's hands on my body, rough and strong. I could go for letting my mind be silent, for the body taking over...

But I can't get into that. Not right now, and maybe not ever, if I want to keep him safe. And I know, in this instant, that I would never forgive myself if something happened to Ben.

He doesn't know it, but it's a risk being in my orbit. People think of orbits as steady, stable, but the truth is that planets wobble off their paths and crash into the sun in a deadly blaze all the time.

"More practical, on-the-ground solutions," he contin-ues, and "*on the ground*" sounds exactly like "*bent over the bed."* "How much left do you have to write? What kind of article is it?"

"It's not an article." A strange laugh escapes me. "It might be easier if it were an article."

"What is it, then?" Ben furrows his brow. "A blog post or something?"

"It's a book. I write books."

His face opens with a delight I'm very familiar with seeing in other people's expressions. "What kind of books?"

"Thrillers." I run a nervous hand through my hair. Another wave of desperation rises, tidal and inexorable, and I take another gulp of air and try to swallow it down. "I write psychological thrillers."

Ben nods, and I can tell just from the set of his face that he wants to ask a thousand questions about this. Most people do, when I tell them what I do for a living. But the man isn't just sexy. He's aware of other people around him, which is a rare find in the men of Manhattan. "So, you're almost at the end of the book, and—"

That makes me laugh. It makes me laugh hard, so hard that after a moment, Ben's serious, helpful expression cracks into a smile like a sunrise, and then the low rumble of his laughter joins mine. Stray tears leak from the corners of my eyes, and I brush them away, careful not to disturb the makeup I applied for the special occasion of having Ben Powell over to my apartment. I take a deep breath, and then another, fighting off another laughing fit.

"Oh, no," I tell him, when I've finally regained the power of speech. "No, it's much, *much* worse than that."

6

BENNETT

Eva is smiling, but her big green eyes show nothing but a fear so strong it borders on panic. Even so, she keeps a little natural grin on her face as if this is all a big joke, though *"it's much, much worse than that"* sounds too serious for smiling. Between getting her text and showing up at her apartment, I only had time to research what I thought was the probable cause of that tension she carries around in her shoulders, so I have no idea what she means. And for some reason, I thought she wrote short articles, not books.

"Are you sure this isn't a matter of perspective?" I say it carefully, because I'm not a complete fucking prick and she didn't text me to hear that it's all in her head. I'm genuinely curious. Morbidly curious, to be totally accurate. But if it's really that world-ending...

Eva shakes her head, still smiling, and it breaks my heart a little, how hard she's trying to hold it together. Clearly, this is getting to her, and it's been getting to her for more than the weekend. "Isn't everything a matter of perspective?"

"Touché."

She draws in a long, slow breath and lets it out then casually wanders toward the window. It seems like an old habit, and it's a good one, because she looks stunning bathed in the city's ambient light. Her entire apartment is like a photography studio, all white walls and neutral furniture and low, low lamps that cast a warm glow over the space. It's almost as if she wanted to keep it clean and boring so that all the excitement could come out in her writing. But what do I know? My apartment's painted white too, and it's only because it was like that when I moved in.

"No, there are some...unavoidable facts in play." Then she narrows her eyes, glancing across at me with a look that burns. "Don't get all hot and bothered. I know that word does it for you." She must be trying to torture me, because she says it again. "Facts."

It catches me off guard, her little joke in the middle of what's clearly some breath-stopping fear, and I can't hide the laugh that escapes my. My heart turns and twists and falls a little more. Not that I can ever really fall in love with Eva. I can be intrigued with her, I can want her, but I can't get carried away. Eventually, she'll discover I'm not the kind of man she wants. That what I need for my own life will always take me away from her. That's how it always goes. But for now....

"I'll try to keep my dick in my pants."

Now it's *her* turn to laugh again, giggles bubbling up and out, her body shaking with them. "Oh, God, don't...don't set me off again. I can't spend the rest of my energy laughing if I'm going to fix this today. Which, you know, I have to. I have to take some action toward fixing the enormous problem I've caused." She says this last bit quietly, and I hear there are two layers of meaning there. I'm not sure what either of them are.

I arrange my face into a stoic expression. "Let's focus here, Eva." She struggles to look serious, too. "You don't know the ending of your book?"

She wriggles her shoulders and sighs like a woman at the end of a hot yoga class. "The ending is the least of my worries."

"So you *know* the ending." I try to force my mind away from how gorgeous she is and how much I want to touch her. "I'm guessing that's the most important thing in a thriller, so if you have that—"

"I don't know the ending. I haven't started yet."

I'm missing some key pieces of information here, and it makes my blood run hot. That's a bigger deal than I thought, and it explains why she's making a last-ditch effort to fix it at ten o'clock at night. I do my best work in the early hours of the morning or when the clock is ticking toward midnight. But then...my work isn't creating entire books from nothing.

"You haven't written any of the book yet?"

"Not one word."

I get it. I get why, as a writer, she'd be under so much stress to meet her deadlines. But a book must take weeks to write. Maybe even months. The dots aren't connecting. Most of the writers I've met in my life do it on the side, not as their main career, so missing a deadline now and then is the cost of doing business.

So it's different for Eva.

"And someone has already paid you for this book?"

She laughs again, a choked little thing. "Oh, yeah. They've paid me. They've paid me so much."

Who *is* this woman? The surface of my skin is alive with the mystery of her, hairs rising on the backs of my arms. Whit said she was a writer, but this seems like...more than that.

"Hey, Eva."

"Yeah?" She raises her eyebrows, hopeful and suspicious all at once.

"Who...are you?"

Eva narrows her eyes, and then I see understanding flicker into her face. "See, if I tell you, this is all going to be ruined."

"Not possible. I'm already ruined."

"How?"

"You slept in my bed last night."

Eva blushes. "And that was enough to—"

"I don't invite just anyone to sleep in my bed."

"Only failed authors, right?"

How can she be a failed author if she's already been paid for it? Eva's apartment is nice enough that she either has lots of money squirreled away somewhere or she got a pretty hefty advance, or both. "Are you a failed author?" Or, I think, some kind of secret heiress? A socialite of some kind?

"No!" She turns away from me, takes three big strides across the living room, and falls onto the couch. I get a flash of her black panties before she smooths the skirt of her dress over her legs, staring at the ceiling. I'm hard as a rock as I follow her.

I want to lean over her, covering her entire body with mine, and kiss her until all the worry is gone from her eyes. I settle for sitting on the nearby loveseat instead. Eva throws her arms over her eyes and breathes deeply.

"You're cute as hell," I tell her. "But if this is a booty call, you can admit it at any time and we can move past—"

"It's not a booty call." Another deep breath in and out. "I'm not a failed author. I'm really, really successful. I'm so successful, Ben. You have no idea."

"Give me an idea."

I have *plenty* of ideas. But none of them, in this moment, would be any help to her. Not with writing the book, anyway.

"I normally don't go around saying...." She presses her lips together like this is a huge and terrible secret then flings her arms away from her face and sits up. "You know what? This was a mistake. I shouldn't be saying anything."

She stands up from the sofa and heads around the other side, like she's going to open the door and see me out, but I'm faster. I go around the back and stand in her path. Eva keeps coming, but before she can brush past, I hook my arm around her waist.

It's just like last night. She leans toward me, instead of away, and her body relaxes. "I'm not leaving that easily." Her eyes are so bright, so green. "Who are you?"

"I'm...." She shakes her head. "I really shouldn't."

"Look." It takes everything I have to string the words together in my mind before I say them, because she's so warm in my arms, and I'm making contact with curves that I would kill to see naked in broad daylight. "If you're a serial killer, I'm already screwed."

She hesitates again, a little laugh, and then, "I'm J. Beckett."

I look down at her.

Is it...another joke? Is this name supposed to mean something? The sound of it tugs at one of the wires in the back of my mind, a memory coming to the surface.

It's almost meaningless, what I remember. I'd been riding the subway to the support group and the people-watching had been fucking terrible. I got sick of staring at my own lap and glanced over the ads. There was one for a book called *The Miracle Girl.*

By one J. Beckett.

A New York Times bestseller.

The cover had been up there next to someone's review —I can't remember whose—but I can remember it said *"Deliciously terrifying and utterly unforgettable."*

She's not some struggling author. J. Beckett is *huge.* The ads on the subway aren't the only things I've seen, now that I think about it. Bookstores have copies of that book in the front window and it came out a year ago. It's one of those books that's destined to be a classic, or at least obnoxiously popular for a good long time. I wonder if she's already sold the movie rights. She probably has. But the Eva standing in front of me is never going to be able to sit down for one of those chummy interviews with the author they put in the bonus content for the DVD release.

"You're J. Beckett," I say stupidly.

"Yes." Eva rests a hand tentatively on my bicep, and I'll

be damned if I'm going to step away, even though the discovery of this is like a mini-high and the adrenaline is making me want to pace around, walk it off a little bit. "I'm J. Beckett. That's my pen name."

"And you can't write."

"I haven't been able to write the next book."

"Why not?"

"I don't know. And they've already paid me a shitload of money for it. I've had months to finish it, and I haven't even started." The last traces of her smile fall away from her face. "The deadline is coming up in three weeks and I have nothing to show for it. I..." Color floods her cheeks. "I've been lying to my editor."

"Can you..." My mind is caught in the maze of the problem, and at every turn, I run into dead ends. Why can't she write? What's stopping her now? Did something happen to her last year to shut her down like this?

How the hell can I get her to tell me about it without having her pull away?

I want her body next to mine almost more than I want to know what the fuck is up with Eva Lipton, who is also J. Beckett, who is the country's darling when it comes to the kind of books that are flying off the shelves right now. I can't believe I never saw her picture before. I *also* can't believe Whitney didn't mention this little detail. "Can you tell them the truth? Let them know what your needs—"

"My needs are not...." Her hand tenses on my arm and Eva turns her face away from the light, into a shadow that makes her green eyes look dim. "I'm not going to call my editor and say "'I'm *sorry. I'm too stupid to think of an idea for this book. I haven't written anything. I can't do this.'* I can't say that." She takes a deep breath and it does nothing to calm her. "You don't have a clue, Ben. You have no idea what kind of risk I'd be running if I did that. You think I can take that chance? I can't take that fucking chance, okay? I can't—"

She's winding herself tighter and tighter, and I know right now that if I let this continue, Eva's going to snap.

There's only one way to stop this.

7

EVA

BEN LEANS in and kisses me, stemming the tide of total nonsense coming from my mouth and swallowing it so tenderly that tears spring to the corners of my eyes. It's oddly...centering, like a good turn with that meditation app on my phone, but it feels a thousand times better than that. A million times better.

I melt into it, my body into his, gripping that firm bicep. There's so much pleasure in his hands on my hips. So much pleasure in the way he tugs me closer, against the bulge of him in his pants. I can taste need like electricity on his tongue and it's a flavor so fine and sharp that I moan into his mouth.

The tenderness ebbs away and he ramps up into a hot, hard possession, and oh my God, oh my God, he's really kissing me like this. Like a man who's lost control. He's yanked me bodily away from all my spiraling anxiety. He's cut it off at the neck. I don't feel anything but those hands, that body....

God, he's hot. I knew it when I first saw him, but touching is believing. And I believe now that Bennett Powell is the sexiest, most magnetic man I've ever met in my life.

I have to breathe, but I don't want to come up for air. I tear myself away from the kiss and gasp in a single, deep breath, my mind clearing for an instant with the influx of oxygen. But then I see his lips, see his eyes searching mine, and it's all over again. I curl my arms around his neck and pull him closer. I'll do anything to keep him near me. I'll do anything for more of this.

He makes an approving noise in the back of his throat that I feel all the way down to my core and between my legs. Jesus, he's hot. He's so hot, and it's making me hot, and wet. I step my legs apart, just in case, *just in case.* If he touched me there, I would allow it. I would love it. I want it—

Ben pulls back.

He does it agonizingly slowly, like he's putting on the brakes on an icy road, and by the time his lips leave mine, I can tell my face must be the color of a Valentine's card. "Why? *Why?*" I breathe, and those brown eyes lock on mine. Nobody looks at me like this. Nobody. Not the reporters who have interviewed me, not the photographers who take my headshots for the book jacket...no one.

"Why what?"

The entire world has shrunk to his thumbs moving slowly up and down on my hipbones and the sound of his voice.

"Why did you stop?"

"Just being a gentleman." His mouth curls in a smile that is the most ungentlemanly thing I've ever seen. "Any other questions?"

"Why did you *start?*" My heart is beating fast, a startled rabbit in my chest.

He has an answer. Of course he has an answer. "The articles I read suggested that touch could have—" He laughs. "—a calming influence and give the...receiver...a rush of endorphins, which might overpower—"

I shake my head, cutting him off. "How much did you research this?"

"I spent the subway ride looking up everything I could."

"And that's why you kissed me?"

He shakes his head. "I kissed you because you're fucking gorgeous. And you smell like springtime. And..."

Ben's watching me, as though he needs visual confirmation of every breath I take. It doesn't seem to matter that he can feel it beneath his hands. "And what?"

"You needed it."

I lean into him, giving a little more of myself over. "How would you know that?"

"I can see your face."

That's what makes his gaze too intense to hold for another moment and I look down. It's a little less like looking into the sun this way, and part of me—a small part—would like it if he let me retreat back into myself. To hide.

He doesn't.

Ben puts his fingers underneath my chin and tilts my face back to his. "I see you," he says, and in the low rumble of his tone, it doesn't seem like some stupid pick-up line. It's the truth, clear and bright as day.

"I don't...I don't know how I feel about that," I admit. "That's not something I want—" My throat tightens. I'm tiptoeing too close to the grief that underpins all of my life, and I can't go there. Not now. Not with my career on the line, and Ben Powell in my apartment. Not with the night wide open like this.

"Why don't you want people to see you?" Ben's voice is pure curiosity and it's like cold water against my skin. "You're successful. Isn't that the cost of doing business?"

I swallow around a painful knot in my throat, and even though I don't want to, even though I want to stay as close to him as I can, in the afterglow of his kiss, I feel myself pulling away. No. *No.* I hold myself as still as I can. Something in the air between us shifts. "There is a cost," I tell him uselessly. I know if I say one more word about it, he'll sense the loose thread that leads into the very heart of me and tug on it until I'm unraveled before him.

It could be a relief, to let him in.

To let him *all* the way in.

But even as I consider it, a warning bell clings in the back of my mind. If Ben finds out what happened, there's no telling what he might think of me. I'd rather him think I'm just your regular anxiety-ridden writer than find the truth.

My heart twists with the guilt. This—this is what I write into all my books. I hide the truth of the stories behind other problems, behind other stories, so that when the curtain draws back, the audience gasps with horror and delight.

I don't want that from Ben.

I go to pull away—really, this time—and he holds me in place.

"Eva."

"Yeah?"

"I'm not going to ask you to stay this time," he says. "I'm going to ask you to leave."

I HAVE NOTHING TO LOSE.

Other than everything.

An hour after Ben suggests he's going to kick me out of my own apartment, we're cruising up the highway to the part of New York that nobody knows about and nobody cares about, except for the people who want to vacation there.

It makes no sense, and in the dark, with the headlights illuminating a narrow path in front of us, I'm beyond caring.

I don't even know where we're going.

"You're going to ask me to *leave?*" I'd squeaked, standing in my living room.

"Yes," Ben said, getting that laser-focused look in his eyes. "With me."

Who could resist that magnetic pull?

I'm o for 2.

He whisked me to the nearest Quik Car Rental. Destination: unknown. All I know is that he clicked and swiped on his phone while I threw clothes into a suitcase. Ben has a plan, even if I don't know what the hell it is. He. Has. A. Plan.

I consider pestering him until he gives up the details, but instead, I lean my head against the headrest and watch the silhouettes of the trees whiz by against the navy sky. I visualize pinning each one of my worries to the trunks and leaving them behind. *Lying to editor,* reads one of the pinned note. *Keeping this secret from Ben.* That last one shouldn't be such a big deal. I don't *owe* him anything.

That's not true; I owe him a lot. I don't know precisely how much yet, but I'm going to be in his debt.

Whitney wouldn't be friends with a serial killer, anyway. I'm sure of it. Her big personality would flush out the truth long before she invited him to her house for a party. So what else can possibly happen on this mystery trip? I raise my fingertips to my lips and causally brush them across. Another kiss like that, and I might get an idea for a story. It'll probably be at romance, but something is better than nothing.

It does occur to me that *if* Ben is a serial killer and I've just agreed to skip town with him, then I won't have to worry about my deadline. How fucking morbid is that? I don't realize I'm laughing, until Ben asks, "What's funny?"

"Nothing," I tell him.

He clicks his tongue and waits.

"I was thinking that if *you're* the serial killer, then I won't have to face the consequences of lying to my editor."

Ben's laughter is full of warmth. "Sorry to disappoint." It must be the excitement, the adrenaline of getting out of town in the middle of the night, that's keeping me awake without a hint of irritation. In fact, I feel more refreshed than I have in weeks, out here on this pitch-black highway lined with trees.

"Only time will tell." I look at him now in the glow of the radio panel. His eyes are on the road, and his hands are steady on the wheel.

I see the flicker of his eyelashes when he glances over at me. "Why did you pick your job?"

Not: when did you know you first loved writing? Not: when did you know that writing was going to be your calling?

"That's not how people usually ask that."

A shadowy smile. "It's how I asked it."

"The answer isn't interesting. It's...pretty boring, actually."

"I'll be the judge of that." Ben changes lanes to pass

some other car that's trundling along well below the speed limit. He's a smooth, careful driver, but being in the car with him is still giving me a head rush.

"I picked this job, because it seemed safe."

"Does it?" He turns his head a fraction of an inch, another look, and then his eyes are back on the road. "You don't act like it's a safe job. You're like a five-alarm fire. Most of the time." If he's thinking about that kiss, he's not the only one.

"I'm in a situation right now." I'm in two situations right now. I'm in a situation with my non-existent book, and a situation with my *very* existent...I don't know what to call him. A crush? A friend? Neither one seems adequate.

"A deadline situation, though. That's not an actual deadline, is it?" Ben shifts in his seat. "If you don't finish the book...?"

The question makes my heart leap up into my throat, makes my lungs feel constricted. I take in a deep breath and let it out. "You never know which things are actual deadlines."

It's a misstep, and I know it. I'm baiting him, and Ben's the kind of guy who will take the bait. He's going to want to know what I'm talking about, and with those eyes on mine, and his hands on my skin, how can I deny him?

Do I even *want* to deny him?

I look back out the window at the trees, a dark blur at ground level as we speed by, lit for a moment each by the edges of the headlights. And I can feel that he's looking at me. Any moment now, he'll ask the question, and I need to make a choice.

Will I give him the answer?

Or will I keep it buried deep down, where it can't hurt anyone else?

An electric anticipation arcs over my skin. This could be the moment when I reveal everything. It could be the moment—

The GPS on his phone lets out a cheery chime.

"In five hundred feet," a woman's voice says, smooth and clear and definitely not hiding anything, "take the next exit."

"Saved by the bell," says Ben.

8

I'VE STAYED HERE BEFORE, so I recognize the turnoff. It's the kind of thing you could easily miss in the dark. This late at night, it almost seems possible that the entire place could have disappeared, so I'm relieved when I see it.

This is my favorite work getaway, which is why I think it'll be perfect for Eva.

It's on the cheap side of a nice lake and it has wireless internet, so when I need to get out of the city and concentrate on work, I'll get it for a week. Right now, I *do* need to concentrate on work. There is a project for the job that pays me hanging over my head. And my secondary job—the one I haven't told Eva about—is nagging at me. When it starts to nag at me like this, I have to shut everything out and focus on it until it releases its grip.

"Where are we?" Eva asks when the cabin comes into view. It doesn't look like much from the outside, but the owners renovated the inside a couple of years ago to nearly the standard of a hotel. Except it's cleaner.

"My favorite getaway."

"Are you going to show me where the bodies are buried?" Eva jokes.

"Bodies would *really* fuck up my peace and serenity," I tell her.

We park in the front and I haul both our bags out of the backseat. At the door, I punch in a code on a little lockbox, which pops open to reveal the key.

Inside, Eva lets out an audible sigh. "Oh, thank God," she says. "I hate camping."

I laugh out loud. "Do you think I'd really take you camping with only a couple bags of clothes?"

She shrugs. "I don't know. You were in the army, so maybe you still have a taste for sleeping on the ground and being uncomfortable."

"Not tonight I don't."

I give her a quick tour. There's a large bedroom with an en suite bathroom, a smaller bedroom with a screened-in porch, and the main area with the living room and kitchen.

It's late as hell when we finally drop our bags in the master bedroom. Eva yawns then bends down and digs through hers until she comes up with a toothbrush and tube of toothpaste.

"Okay, so." She stops herself, watching me, and her shyness makes me hard as a rock. "We've already slept in the same bed before—"

"And you found it mortifying."

"And I did find it mortifying, yes." She tugs her bottom lip between her teeth.

"But you also loved it."

Desire flashes through Eva's eyes, but a yawn comes right on its heels.

"I missed it when it was over," she admits quietly.

"Enough that you'd risk coming to a deserted cabin with a serial killer?"

She laughs. "Honestly, I think I'm the better candidate for serial killer." Eva blushes, and it's the prettiest thing

I've ever seen. Just like every other time. "Don't make me ask for it."

There are *so* many things I'd like to make her beg for that it hurts me. My cock is painfully hard. But I can see the slope of her shoulders and the burn in her eyes.

I'll let her off the hook. This time.

"Want to sleep in my bed, Eva?"

"It sounds so dirty when you say it like that." She makes her way past me, brushing close.

"I can sound dirtier," I call after her as she disappears into the bedroom.

Eva pokes her head back out, exhaustion written on her face alongside pleasure. "Don't tempt me."

WE GET into bed and I'm thinking of tempting her. I'm thinking of reaching over and pushing down her little shorts she's wearing. She changed into them in the bathroom, leaving the book dress behind. I'm absolutely certain that her body would react in *very* pleasant ways. But it's the middle of the night, and as intoxicating as she is, I shouldn't....

I shouldn't is the last thought that crosses my mind for the rest of the night. With her warm body curled next to mine, breathing gentle and slow, I sleep as deeply as I ever have since I came back from Afghanistan. Eva's the one who thinks she needs me to get her out of her situation, but I'm beginning to think it's the other way around.

Not that I'm going to put that on her. Not now, and maybe not ever.

I wake up when the sun hits my face through the slats in the newly installed wooden blinds.

Eva isn't next to me.

She's already up, standing at the window, staring at the lake, her ass mind-numbingly perfect in those little shorts.

I turn over, pulling up the sheets to hide what we *all* know is going on beneath them, and she turns to face me, a sleepy grin on her face. "It's beautiful out there. I thought we were in the middle of nowhere. Like, actual serial killer territory."

"That would suck on a first date."

She lets out a little huff of a laugh. "Isn't this our second date?"

"I think the first one was a one-night stand."

Eva frowns. "How can it be a one-night stand if I'm in this cabin with you right now?"

"You're right." I run a hand over my face. "It'll be a three-night stand at least."

She considers me carefully. "Is this part of your writer's block solution?"

"Could be. Being out here, it gets the blood flowing."

"I can think of other ways to get the blood flowing." She says it half under her breath, almost to herself.

"What was that?" I cup a hand to my ear. I would *really* like to hear her say it louder.

"Nothing." Eva gives me a bratty little grin and heads for the bathroom.

I do several deep-breathing exercises while the water runs so that I'm not at full attention when she emerges. Before she does, I go and knock on the bathroom door. "Did you bring a bathing suit?"

There's a sudden hush from inside.

"Eva?"

"Yeah, I brought one." Her voice is a little tight. "Are you planning to look at me wearing it?"

"What in the hell kind of question is that?"

Eva pulls open the door and crosses the room to her bag. It gives me a mild heart attack when she bends over to rifle through the contents. "Hang on."

Then she goes back into the bathroom, shutting the door tightly and locking it.

As if I'd barge in while she was changing like some animal.

I go down the hall to the other bathroom with my suit, and when I come back, she's standing in the middle of the bedroom.

"My God." It takes all my willpower not to bend her over the bed right then.

"Don't," she says, face red. "This is...it's from a billion years ago. I keep it in this travel bag, and it's not like I knew we were going to be swimming—"

"Stop."

I can't listen to her protest. Not when I'm looking at one of God's very best masterpieces.

The bikini *barely* fits.

Or...it fits her too well.

It fits her *indecently* well.

"Yeah," I say finally. "I'm planning to look at you."

"Ben, it's..." She gestures to her breasts, which are *this close* to spilling out of the damn thing. I'd untie it right now if I wasn't trying to be a decent person. "It's like this."

"There's nobody else around," I reply crisply. Anyway, they're more likely to notice the bulge in the front of my bathing suit. It's working out as well as Eva's. "Let's do it."

Eva follows me through the house and then we go out across the green, tended lawn toward the narrow beach. The sand here is pretty fucking pristine for the cheap side of the lake, and watching her hips sway as she walks is nearly my undoing.

It's a clear morning, though already warm and humid, and my toes sink into the sand on the way to the water's edge. Eva wonders out loud if it's going to be cold.

"I hope it'll be cold."

She whips her head around and looks at me, eyes dancing. "Perv."

"For maximum refreshment."

"Hardly."

"Maximum shrinkage, more like."

This makes me laugh, but it also makes me slightly self-conscious. Not that it'll matter mid-swim.

It really is nice here. Eva shades her eyes with her hand and turns back to the water, a little smile on her face.

There's a red buoy bobbing way out in the lake, and the sand is warm between my toes. Nothing like the fine, gritty bullshit in Afghanistan. Eva drops her towel heavily to the ground and stretches her arms over her head, the old bikini rising up a little bit to show another inch of the curve of her breast.

I can't take it.

So I suck in a deep breath and do a little hop on the sand.

Eva looks at me like I'm crazy. "You're not serious. You don't want to wade in first? Ease into the morning?"

"Dead serious." I want to rush into the water. I want to

rush all the walls she has up around her, and learn all her secrets. I want to have all of her in my hands. And if I can't do that, then I'm going to go around the side and challenge her. Bit by bit. "Are you a good swimmer?"

"I'm fine, but—"

"No buts. First to the buoy and back wins. One, two, three, *go*."

I sprint for the water, and there's a moment when I think she might just stay on the sand, laughing, but with a shriek, she follows me in. The water hits my knees—it's cold; *fuck*, it's cold—and my head clears just in time for me to dive into the shallows.

When I resurface, the first thing I see is Eva kicking hard alongside me, taking the lead.

She's fine at swimming. Sure.

In fact, she's lighter and leaner and moves through the water like a fish, like a mermaid, and my lungs burn as I try to keep up. And I'm in good fucking shape. We tear through the water and go in opposite directions around the buoy. At the last moment, I think I might crash into her, and Christ would I enjoy that, but Eva dives down deep. The water has to be over her head; it's definitely over mine, but she doesn't seem to care at all. I'm still careening around the buoy when her head breaks the surface, sprinting for shore, arms flying, water droplets bright as diamonds in the sun.

The shore has never seemed so close and so far at the same time.

I'm close enough to reach out and grab her ankle, but she's kicking so powerfully I don't even begin to dare. I push harder, lungs screaming, water fighting back, and we both pop up out of the lake at the same time. Eva runs through the water, knees high. "I won!" she shouts breathlessly, turning to point at me. "I won!"

Her bikini top has ridden up over one peaked nipple, her cheeks are pink, and she looks so fucking radiantly happy, her hair dripping wet. She's *beaming*. It's not a conscious decision I make—I realize that—because the next thing I know, we're running toward each other through the water. I hate it, a little bit, for dragging me back.

But the collision—holy God, it's glorious. All wet skin and slipping suits, and I reach down and tug the bikini down. Eva squeals, feeling what I'm doing, and my lips are on hers. She tastes like toothpaste and victory, and she's kissing me back so hard it verges on a bite. How risky would it be to fuck her on the sand, on a towel, right here?

Somebody whistles.

It sounds close enough to be right behind me, but when I turn around, it's three guys in a fishing boat, the sound carrying over the water. They're out past the buoy, shouting and cheering and catcalling. "We see you!" The moment the sound hits us, Eva flinches away from me, her hand going to her mouth, the sound of her legs moving through the water one of the sadder things in my life.

Mood shattered.

I go after her and the guys on the boat clap, the sound echoing off the cabin, and I no longer give a shit what they're saying. Eva moves fast across the sand to her towel, snatches it up, and shakes it out. Then she wraps it around herself like it's chainmail. One stony glance back out at the guys in the boat and she heads for the cabin.

I sweep up my own towel at a run and manage to catch her by the elbow. My heart is still pounding with the effort of the swim. "What's wrong?"

She puts on a smile as fake as I've ever seen. "I'm

supposed to be working, right? Writing. That's why you brought me here."

"That's one reason, but it's not—"

"I'll race you," she says quickly, the smile shifting, becoming genuine.

"Race me to what? The cabin's fifteen feet away."

Eva looks up into my face. "You must have work, too. I saw your laptop bag. What kind of job is it?" Another thought crosses her mind. "It's Sunday, so you must... you must work online, or from home."

"I'm a fact-checker." The actual title is fancier than that, but it doesn't matter. And it's not the whole truth, but...that's for another time.

"So I'll race you." Eva's eyes are bright. "I'll get *something* done, before you can, or else...."

"Or else winner takes all."

Eva stops dead and searches my eyes.

I'm serious.

"Deal," she says.

I MIGHT HAVE OVERREACTED to the guys on the boat.

Okay. I *definitely* overreacted to the guys on the boat.

They were just a collection of human assholes out to have a nice fishing trip. And who knows? Maybe they were trying to applaud our human resiliency. It's not easy to make out like that after an intense competition.

I overreacted, but it was such a sudden reminder of the consequences. Which, honestly, could be pretty devastating. Life has taught me that much.

And now I've challenged Ben to a writer's retreat.

I've never been on a writer's retreat before. My agent has fielded a few invites for me and so has my editor, but I've never gone. I know how women can get, late at night when the wine is flowing, and I don't have a story to tell. No, I have a story to tell. It's not one I want to speak out loud, late at night when the wine is flowing. It's too heavy for moments like that. And then... what happens then? It brings everybody together. You let people in. And once they're close to me, who knows what could happen?

This is a huge reason why I moved to New York City. It's huge and anonymous and the odds that I might meet someone are slim. I don't know what's worse, actually. Getting bogged down with someone who only wants me for my success—which, ha—or falling for someone it'll hurt like death itself to lose.

Not to mention Bennett, and his eyes on me, and his hands on me, and the way he kisses me like we might never kiss again.

Well. I've challenged him to a work race, and now I'm going to deliver. I saw the look in those eyes when he said *winner takes all*.

I press my thighs together, denim between my legs. I went directly inside the cabin and changed into a light off-the-shoulder sweatshirt over my favorite tank top and a pair of denim cutoffs. All of it is comfortable enough to write in. And, after running into the water like that, my head is clearer than it's been in months.

It's easier to think out here, away from the city.

In one way.

But in another way...

The thought of Bennett inside the house makes my skin heat. The way his fingers brushed over my nipple when he tugged my suit down for me, it makes me lightheaded. He could have torn it off, for all I cared in that moment, but instead, he shielded me from additional embarrassment. Those guys on the boat would have *loved* that.

And...

I want to see what it means when he's the winner. I want to see what it means when he takes all. But then I'd have to give in, and giving in like that is hard to face. The thought of letting someone get *that* close, so close they could see all the terrible things about me....

I've got to focus.

I sit up straight and open a fresh Word document.

I normally write in a separate program, but seeing the icon makes me anxious, so it's back to the basics. My meditation app on my phone would tell me to look gently upon my surroundings, so I take a deep breath in, let it out, and consider the lawn.

It really is beautiful here. The neatly tended grass. The thin strip of clean sand, and the blue water. Another fishing boat trawls by out in the deep, but it looks like one guy is in it, and from this distance it seems almost peaceful. The summer breeze stirs my hair, and—as the app would also tell me to do—I feel the weight of my body in the chair, which is also connected to the earth. As lawn chairs go, this one is pretty nice. If I had a balcony back at my apartment, I might even get one to put out there.

Or I could keep coming here with Bennett.

Recognize the thought and let it go.

Focus.

I bring my eyes peacefully back to my laptop screen and put my fingers to the keyboard.

I've got to write something. That's the entire point of this. I asked Bennett for help with writer's block, and he pulled a white knight and whisked me away to a secret fortress in the form of a summer cabin. And if I can work here, if I can get *something* on paper, I can flesh out the story I've been telling Kayla, my editor. She's a pretty no-nonsense person. Good to the bone, and hilarious too. A consummate professional. But she's going to be pissed about the fact that I lied to her this entire time. The only thing to do now is turn it into a little bit less of a lie.

Shit.

How do I do this? I've written two books so far, and started a lot of others, and every time I start a new book, I feel completely virginal and incapable of figuring out the basics.

What I need is an ending. In this way, Ben was right. If I know the ending, I could work backward to the beginning. But in order to know the ending, I need to know who's involved, which circles me right back to the beginning.

I close my eyes and focus on my breath. My mind quickly wanders away to the sound of the wind chime on the breeze, the waves lapping at the sand, and—is that Bennett typing inside? He's definitely beating me. Is he also looking at me? I love the way this sweatshirt makes my shoulders look. He'd probably want to tug it down to see more, and in the process, he could plant a kiss against my collarbone. And then he'd look at me, with those coppery brown eyes, and he would see everything I needed. I wouldn't need to say a single word. He'd lift me in those muscled arms of his, and we would not pass go, we would not collect two hundred dollars, we would proceed directly to bed.

Which is not the beginning of a thriller. With Ben, it's the beginning of a romance novel. If I could get out of my own way and let it happen.

I hope he can't see me right now. My breath has gone quick and shallow, and I open my eyes and stare out at the water.

Imagine being plunged into cold water, I tell myself firmly. *Like before, when you and Ben were—*

Everything leads back to him.

If Whitney were here, she would look at me with that expression of hers that says *Eva, the world is but a circus, and we are players in it* or some other weird saying, but the conversation would end with her telling me to take Bennett Powell to bed, in no uncertain terms.

And I would.

Except I challenged him to a race that I'm currently losing.

See? This is what happens when you're high on victory. You end up practically jumping a guy in the middle of the lake, and then some asshole in a boat interrupts you, and then you have to rechallenge him again to something you're no question going to lose.

I grit my teeth and close my eyes again.

A character. Any character. Any woman, really. I tend to write about women finding themselves in extraordinarily bad situations.

Hello? I call into the writer's blocked reaches of my mind. *I would really like to see where things go with Bennett, and I can't unless a character shows up* right now.

And just like that, there she is.

A woman who looks like me, only she has long, chestnut locks.

Like my sister had.

She *could* be me, if it weren't for the hair, and the eyes. The shape of our faces would be similar.

But she's not me.

She's looking for something, and that search will take her into danger. A danger that will make my readers' hearts pound with fear for her. And why is she looking? Go back, go back.

She needs the money.

A student, maybe.

Now she has a backpack slung over one shoulder.

A college student. Alone. And why is she alone? Why can't she ask her family for the money?

No family.

Now we're getting somewhere.

In a burst of inspiration, I write **Chapter One** at the top of the document.

Well, maybe she does have a family. I don't know. My last heroine didn't have a dad.

I've never subscribed to the wisdom that a person should write only what they know. My life has never been like a psychological thriller, except for one similarity, which isn't really a similarity to thrillers. It's just how life is.

Suddenly, I'm wending my way down a train of thought involving life imitating art and art imitating life, and I jump when the door of the cabin slams open behind me.

Footsteps muffled by the grass.

And then Ben comes into view with a triumphant grin on his face.

"I win."

10

BENNETT

SHE FREEZES, going absolutely still except for the loose strands of hair floating on the breeze. Maybe we've gone as far as this little game is going to take us. Maybe we're on the verge of something else entirely. So many things are flashing through her green eyes that I can't pin any one of them down.

Eva takes in a breath, shallow and quick, and then I see it.

Excitement.

This can go one of two ways.

I lay down another challenge. Another chance for her to claim victory, if she can. Or admit defeat, if that's how she wants to play this.

Personally, I hope she goes down fighting.

"Here's what I've done." I open my own laptop and flip the screen toward her. My submitted assignment for this week's project has been date-stamped. "Show me yours." I crack a smile that has a deep blush covering her cheeks in an instant. "It's only fair."

Eva screws her mouth up into something between a smirk and a pout and turns her screen toward mine.

On the screen is a Word document.

At the top of the page, she's written **Chapter One.**

That's all.

"Seen enough yet?" Eva asks, her voice high and tight.

"I haven't seen *nearly* enough." I close her laptop with one hand and put mine on top of it, and then I place both palms on the arms of the lawn chair. I lean in *close.* Close enough to smell her shampoo and the sunscreen she carefully applied before she came out here in that little bikini. Close enough that I can hear her short little breaths, almost panting, when I murmur our agreement into her ear. "Winner takes all."

"Where are you going to take me?"

I let my breath play over the shell of her ear and watch

the tilt of her head, almost imperceptible, toward my lips.

And then I give her the answer.

"Lunch."

EVA'S GIDDY, a sparkling energy settling over her skin. She leans back in the passenger seat of the rental car and puts her bare feet up on the dash. I don't know if she's relieved that I haven't taken her to bed or impatient for it. Knowing what I know of her, it's a combination of both.

But first, we have to eat.

There's a tiny-ass town fifteen minutes down the road. The lake sits up high, surrounded by hills, so we follow their natural curves through deep woods. My phone goes in and out of service, so I'm relying on road signs to get us there.

A break in the trees gives us a stunning view of the lake, all diamond lights flickering on the surface, and Eva gasps. "Look at that!"

She points, and I steal a quick glance.

It's a regatta, a bunch of sailboats skimming over the deep water.

She cranes her neck and presses her face to the window as if that'll help her see through the trees. "Oh, that is such a *sight*," Eva says. "All of them chasing each other like that."

It's weird, the things she's delighted by, but what the hell? If she wants to find joy in watching these boats rush across the lake, then I won't stand in her way. She's *got* to relax if she's going to get anywhere with her book.

Or with me.

At the next break in the trees, I pull off the road. It's a wide shoulder, not exactly a roadside stop, but there's enough room for our car, plus a guardrail to lean on.

"Are you stopping?" Eva asks, even though clearly, I am.

"Don't you want to see who wins the race?"

Eva beams at me, clicks the button of her seatbelt, and hops out of the car.

A minute later, we're standing at the guardrail, watching the boats hurtle across our view.

"How are we supposed to know which one is the winner?" Eva asks.

"No idea." She laughs at my answer, and I put my hand on the small of her back. She presses back into my palm and I linger in that little shock of pleasure. "I don't know how they score regattas. All I know is they used to have one every week all summer where I grew up."

I feel her notice that, even if I keep my eyes on the sailboats. Neither of us has offered up much to the other, but here's what I know about getting the facts: you have to be willing to give some up too.

"Where did you grow up?" Eva's tone is cautious, casual, as if she knows where this kind of thing might lead.

We might end up knowing too much about each other.

And as much as I want to postpone the inevitable fallout that will happen when she finally understands how deeply I follow things, I have to know more about her too.

"Michigan. A little town in—"

A truck horn blares not far off, so loud it seems to shake the trees.

Eva whips her head toward the noise. "Way out here?"

"Probably making a delivery to town." I press my hand more firmly into the small of her back. I can hear the truck on the road *now*; I was paying attention to her before. It's heavy, rumbling, and for an instant the noise melds with the sound of that Humvee in Afghanistan. That day, Wes Sullivan was driving, and Dayton Nash was up front with him. We'd been going to scout a village. "Look at those fuckers run," Wes had said shortly before the explosion rocked the front of the Humvee. Dayton lost a leg that day. I lost my ability to focus on anything but getting answers. Why had we been there? Who had planted the IED? It was supposed to be a safe route. Vetted. And it wasn't.

That doesn't matter now. I've worked through that story for long enough that it doesn't pull me under and into the memory. Instead, I'm hyperaware of the differences between then and now. Then, the wheels of the Humvee had kicked up rocks. The road was full of them. Made of them. The truck is on pavement. There's a screech that seems out of place.

I'm on full alert.

The truck isn't in sight, and then the next moment, it is, barreling into view around a sharp turn. The turn had been nothing in the little rental car. But the truck is going too fast.

What the hell?

"Ben," Eva says, and I don't look down at her, because I can't take my eyes off the truck.

The front of it is covered in bugs, and it's filthy, as if the driver got lost on a dirt road and only now found himself out on the little two-lane highway. The sun glints off the windshield, blocking him from view, and then the truck wrenches to the side and I see him.

He has one hand on the wheel, but he's leaned over at a funny angle. Like he's digging for something on the floor.

The man driving the truck has a bloody nose.

It's running down his face and onto the shirt, so he must be grabbing for tissues.

The truck is close enough to see his eyes.

And the look in his eyes is enough to send a wave of ice through my core.

He doesn't see us.

He's not paying attention to the curves in the road, but

he is paying attention to whatever he's trying to find on the floor of the cab. His forehead is wrinkled, but he's looking at something far away.

Fuck. *Fuck.*

Eva gasps, a strangled sound, and the information from my brain finally reaches my muscles.

There's no time.

I wrap my arm around her waist and lift her, throwing us both over the guardrail as the semi rear-ends the little rental car at top speed. The guardrail catches my thigh as we go over, a line of metal and pain against my shorts, and all I know is I can't land on top of her. I shift my weight just in time to take the brunt of the impact.

Thank God, there's not a cliff on the other side of the rail. Just a gentle sloping hill, and I brace my arms so I don't crush Eva. We tumble into a patch of wildflowers.

"Oh, *shit.*" It must be the driver of the semi. "Oh, shit." I look up, and the guy is standing in the middle of the road. The collision carried the little rental car and the cab of the truck across the centerline. He must have overcorrected, and now his semi truck is blocking the entire road. "Fuck!" he shouts, and then he appears at the guardrail. His nose is still bleeding. "Are you guys okay?"

I turn my attention back toward Eva, who is on her back beneath me, wildflowers in her hair.

Her face is an ashen pale, and tears leak from the corners of her eyes.

Oh, Jesus. What if there was something on the ground? What if—

My field training kicks in and I put a hand to the side of her face. "You're okay," I tell her, trying to telegraph as much calm as possible. "I've got you. You're okay, Eva."

I check the front of her clothes for any sign of blood.

There is none.

"Are you okay?" The driver doesn't sound okay. "I'm going to call 9-1-1. Don't worry. I've got it," he calls. "I've got it."

I press my fingers up and down Eva's arms, down to her wrists, to her hands. "Does anything hurt? Eva, tell me if it hurts."

She presses her lips together so tightly they go white.

"Eva," I say firmly. "Are you in any pain?"

She shakes her head.

"Okay. I'm going to turn you over, so I can make sure."

I don't know what I'm expecting when I lift her. A piece of shrapnel jutting out of her back. Something equally horrific.

But when I've cradled her up far enough to see, there's nothing. A few flower petals. A blade of grass.

She's shaking in my arms. Shock? I pull her in tighter. The police will be here any minute, and probably an ambulance, but there's no fucking way in hell I'm letting anyone touch her when she's this terrified. Eva is already coiled tight under the stress of her deadline. The urge to protect her is like a fire raging across the center of my chest. I need to, even though I know a woman like her.... She's stronger than anyone thinks. But why? What made her that way?

Jesus. This is *not* the time to think about this. Not now.

"Hey." I keep my voice even and calm. "We're all right. It didn't touch us."

Eva turns so I can see her face. Her teeth are chattering, and she's still a deathly pale. I can't tell if she knows she's crying or not. I wipe away one tear with the pad of my thumb, and then another. Eva slides her hand up my shirt then grips the fabric in her fist.

Then she uses it to pull herself upright.

Both her hands go to her face, touching her cheeks, her lips, her hair. I smooth my hand over her curls. Tears drip down onto her lap. Eva seems to notice them for the first time, tracing one fingertip over the droplet.

Her eyes move over to my lap.

"Gorgeous." Am I even getting through to her? "We're both fine." I glance back up at the road. "The rental car is a goner, but we can chalk that up to a freak accident." I smile at her, even though my heart is still pounding. "The insurance will cover it."

Eva won't look at me, but she does reach up to brush another teardrop away. "It was…." She swallows hard. "That was so much more terrifying than I imagined it." She moves closer, a subtle shift, and I could die with how much I love that. But her eyes are still on my lap. "And also you're bleeding."

11

EVA

I can't stop seeing it in my mind, over and over. The red cab of the truck coming right at us. The rental car would have crushed us to death before the semi swept it out into the middle of the highway. I saw it when we went over the guardrail, heard it, the screech of metal against metal, sparks flying, the impact right where we'd been standing.

Oh, fuck, it had been so awful. I'll never forget it for the rest of my life. That sharp, wrenching fear. Fuck. *I really might die.* That's what I'd been thinking.

And that was the worst thing of all.

They couldn't have been oblivious. Could they? No. All of them, all three of them, had been awake when it happened, and now I've survived again in a cruel twist of fate.

The knowledge ricochets around underneath my skin like a creature trying to get out. I can feel the shakes, but I can't stop them.

"The paramedics are here," Ben says as he lifts me from the ground and sets me on my feet, holding on a long extra moment to make sure I'm not going to fall over. He ran his hands over my ankles and legs, but he's double-checking to be sure. I'm still busy replaying that near miss in my mind to say anything.

We're walking, and then there are hands and voices helping us step back over the guardrail. Ben must give my name, because the next thing I know, there's a black woman with a smooth voice saying, *"Eva, my name is Natalie, and I'm here to help you,"* and the two of them are ushering me toward the open back of an ambulance.

The antiseptic smell of it hits me like a punch in the face and I rear back into Natalie's arm. Ben reaches out to steady me. "No. Nope. I'm good." It lifts me bodily out of my memory and into the present. And in this present, I am not getting into the back of an ambulance. I am not going to the hospital.

"Ma'am," says the paramedic, Natalie, "you've had a shock, and it'll be best for you if you—"

"I said no," I repeat louder. I don't want either of them to take their hands off me, but I am not going to any hospital. Not today.

I look over my shoulder and catch Natalie exchanging a look with Ben. "Sir, if you and your wife—"

I'll admit it; *wife* sounds nice enough to send a jolt of warmth right through me. But to hell with everyone at this scene if they're going to try to make me go in there. "Ben's not my husband," I say, and it sounds like a lie. "And I'm not going in the ambulance."

Natalie looks at him again, assessing him, and her eyebrows flicker upward in what looks like approval.

"He's going to go home with me," I state. "I mean... he'll take me home." A grin flashes on Ben's face and disappears again. "I'm going home. If you want to check me out, do it right here.

Natalie appraises me, brow furrowed. It's true. I'm not really making the case that I'm fine enough to walk away from the scene. To prove I'm acting in good faith, I plop my ass down on the deck of the ambulance and extend my arm out to her. "Blood pressure. Whatever you want." My teeth are chattering and I clench my jaw to get them to stop.

Natalie reaches into the ambulance behind me and pulls out a blood pressure cuff. She fastens it around my arm. "What's your last name, Eva?"

"Lipton."

"And what day is it?"

I have to think about it. It seems like a million years have passed since I went to the party at Whitney's. "Sunday." She unfastens the cuff and gets out a little penlight.

"Follow the light," she tells me.

"I didn't hit my head," I insist, but I follow the instructions to the letter. "Besides, he's the one bleeding."

Another paramedic is with the driver of the truck. *That* guy is in rough shape. Bloody nose. They've got him sitting on the pavement, and he leans over and throws up onto the ground. Natalie glances over her shoulder. "We've got him covered."

"No. Ben."

He's standing right behind her, probably on purpose,

and the blood from his cut is soaking through his shorts. They're almost too dark for it to be obvious.

Natalie drops her flashlight and reaches for Ben's arm.

Ben shakes his head. "You're sure she's all right?"

She turns back to me. "Eva, can you move over to the side? We need to deal with this cut right now." Her voice is perfectly calm, perfectly even, but I sense a certain urgency.

"Don't bother with me unless she's okay," Ben says. He's resisting Natalie's attempt to get him to sit beside me and I hop up to my feet.

"I'm fine."

He looks me in the eye. "You're not."

"I'll be fine," I tell him.

Another ambulance pulls up, and then a police car.

Natalie pulls up Ben's shorts to expose the cut. The guardrail's edge was sharp enough to go through the fabric. "I bet you're going to refuse to go to the hospital too," she says to Ben.

He's still looking at me when he answers. "I wouldn't leave her for anything."

IT TAKES LONGER than I expected. We both have to give statements to the police, and then a tow truck comes, and then, and then, and then.... They don't force me to go to the hospital, but we have no car. The police chief gives us a ride two towns away so we can replace the rental car, and all I want to do once we're in it is drive back to the cabin.

Eating lunch seems like a bad omen. Ben doesn't fight me on it. His leg is wrapped in gauze and not bleeding anymore. It's funny how shallow cuts can bleed, and bleed like that, and just...stop.

By the time we pull back into the cabin's driveway, it's bathed in the kind of late afternoon light that reminds me of standing at my recital, waiting and waiting as the sun went down. It twists at my heart.

Ben runs a hand through his hair. "Maybe we should—"

"Be alone," I finish for him. "I need to be alone."

"You're sure?"

"Yeah."

I can still hear his words from earlier ringing in my ears. *I wouldn't leave her for anything.*

I feel his eyes on me as I search out the laptop on the counter in the kitchen, pick it up, and go into the second bedroom. He doesn't follow me, but a minute later, I hear him settle into the couch in the living room.

He's not leaving.

But he's seen too much, and I honestly don't know if I can live with it.

THE SECOND BEDROOM leads onto a little screened-in porch, and that's where I perch with my laptop on my lap and look out over the lake.

A storm is coming.

The day was clear this morning, but as the afternoon wears on and I can't bring myself to write anything, a line of dark clouds approaches. They leach the sun out of the sky, coming to cover everything.

Ben doesn't interrupt me.

He doesn't knock on the door, though at some time past

four, I hear him in the kitchen. There's the scrape and clang of pots and pans.

The sky gets darker.

The sun can't have set yet, but the clouds trend toward black. The breeze picks up, becoming a stiff wind, and it whips right through the screen. A strand of hair blows into my eyes. "*Shit*," I hiss under my breath, and get up to shut the glass windows that cover the screen.

It feels urgent now. The air seems to crackle with unshed lightning, and I'm worried for the furniture in here. If the water comes through the screens, it'll be a nightmare to dry out. There are four big glass windows and I pull them shut one by one, and as I flip the lock on the last one, the storm breaks right over the cabin.

Nothing we could do could stop it from coming, and now I have a wild urge to be in it. I push open the screen door and step out into the rain.

It's *pouring*.

It soaks the off-the-shoulder sweatshirt I'm wearing in two seconds, a warm summer thunderstorm verging on cool, and then the water works its way through my shorts. I tilt my face up to the sky and raise my arms toward the rain. I look insane.

Somewhere to the left, off in the woods, there's a *crack* like a shot, ringing with a residual sizzle, and when the answering thunder booms, it's so loud it knocks my teeth together.

"Holy shit," I yell into the storm, for lack of something profound to shout. I can't hear the words as much as I can feel them, and I shout it again just to feel that hum at the center of my body.

"Eva!" Ben's voice cuts through the noise somehow, like he's on another frequency from the rest of the world.

I turn around. He's standing in the open screen door, which is banging against the front of the cabin like it's about to fly off its hinges.

"What are you doing?" He cups his hands around his mouth to make his shout carry.

Another superheated crack of lightning touches down in the woods, and I let the thunder rock through me. "I wanted to feel it," I shout back at him.

"What?"

He comes out from the porch, rushing toward me, and he's instantly soaked to the skin. If *this* is what he looks like in the shower, then this is a sight I want to see every day for the rest of my life.

Ben must like the sight of me too, because he's wearing a half smile by the time he gets to me. He wipes at the rain in his eyes and holds out his hand. "You're going to get struck by lightning."

"I wanted to feel it," I say again.

"Trust me, you *don't* want to get struck by lightning."

"We're surrounded by trees."

"Eva." He laughs. "Narrowly avoiding death by semi didn't do it for you?"

"Not everyone avoids it."

"Okay." He looks at me through the rain and the wind kicks up, slamming the screen door against the side of the cabin. Another crack of lightning, this one closer. "You can tell me all about *whatever the hell it is you're talking about* once we're both inside and not about to get killed by lightning."

"What if it's terrible?"

He reaches out and takes my hand. Ben is muscled, tall, strong; it takes him no effort to pull me in close and wrap his arm around my shoulders. "I'll carry you if I have to."

Suddenly, it hits me—the roiling storm right on top of our heads, the relatively open lawn, the force of the wind. "I can walk," I tell him, but he's already hustling us toward the door.

Three steps inside, he turns back and forces himself out into the rain, pulling the screen door closed. Then he unhooks the latch of the storm door and pushes it firmly closed.

I'm shivering, full-body shakes. Inside, away from the whipping rain, my soaked clothes feel smothering against my skin. This little cabin must have central air, or some kind of A/C unit, because it's *much* cooler inside. Water pools on the floor at my feet.

"Let's go, let's go." Ben says this as urgently as if we're still standing out in the rain. I let him lead me out to the main room, which is half living room, half kitchen, and watch as he opens a closet tucked in next to the cabinets and pulls out one towel, two, and an extra blanket.

"What are you doing?" he asks as puts the bundle of towels and blankets onto the kitchen counter and strips off his shirt. Right *now* what I'm doing is feeling my brain melt at the sight of the most perfect abs I have ever viewed in this or any lifetime. He unbuckles his belt. "Eva?"

I drag my eyes back to his face. "Yeah?"

"It's time to get naked."

12

Eva's face changes as fast as the clouds rolling over us. One minute, she's red as a beet. The next, she's lit up like a shooting star. And then her face goes dark again.

The near miss with the semi shook her to the core. It would shake me too. There's something else there, something beneath the truck that came at us today, but all that matters now is that she's dripping wet.

She looks at me from her place in the middle of the living room, eyes so green it's as if they contained their own living storm. What the hell was she *doing* out there? If she wanted to feel alive, that's one way to do it. But I felt plenty alive after I jumped us over that guardrail.

"Time to get naked," she says softly, and another roll of thunder booms. The rain is so loud on the roof that I can barely make out her words.

"I wouldn't let you sit around in wet clothes any more than I'd have let any vehicle hit you earlier."

There's a flash of lightning in her eyes, and her gaze slips lower, to where my hands are undoing my belt.

The paper-thin sweatshirt is the first to go.

She peels it over her head, revealing a spaghetti strap tank top that's cupping her breasts just like the bikini did.

I drop my pants to the floor and step out of them.

There's no way to be casual about this. I'm hard as a fucking rock, and Eva is still fully clothed.

I'm hyperaware of every breath she takes. Every shift of her weight. Every drip of water from her skin hitting the oval braided rug beneath her feet. Eva drags her bottom lip through her teeth and follows it with the tip of her tongue.

The rain on the roof gets louder.

I don't know how it does, but it's louder. The worst of the storm must be circling right on top of us, and my heart speeds up at the thought of her standing out there in the open, exposed.

I'd rather have her exposed in here.

I cross my arms over my chest and a pure, clean energy fills the room beneath the hammering downpour. Push and pull. A tug of war. I take off my pants and shirt; you give me *something*.

Take off that tank top, I think. *Take it off and show me what's underneath.*

The moment I saw Eva at that party, I knew I couldn't hurry this along. Not that I'm some fucking sicko who gets off on pressuring women into sex. No. That shit is for cowards and assholes and scum. Did it hurt my very skin to sleep in bed with her without even crossing the unspoken line in the center of the bed? Yes, it fucking did. But nothing hurts so good as this.

Eva must see the challenge in my eyes, because there's a little flare of recognition in her eyes, and those full lips turn up at one corner.

Suddenly, she's not a woman in crisis. Right before my eyes, she's made taller and more confident. She's not shying away from my gaze. She's connected to it, reveling in it.

And then she turns around.

I groan out loud, and it's only then that I realize how tightly wound I am.

It shouldn't be possible for the rain to get any louder, for it to beat any more powerfully on the roof of this cabin, but it does. It's so deafening that it sinks its claws into those old memories of explosions in Afghanistan, of that tearing metal blooming beneath our Humvee, and I take all of them in my fists and shove them deep into the reaches of my mind.

I don't have time to think of that right now, because Eva has gripped the hem of her tank top and is wriggling out of it. The wet fabric sticks to her skin. It's possible she's teasing me. It's possible she's taunting me.

It's over her head.

There's no bra underneath.

Eva lets it fall to the floor next to her.

Lightning flashes.

She's silhouetted in front of the giant picture window and the afterimage of the perfect curve of her hips leading to her pert round ass is permanently seared into my memory.

Eva turns, her profile backlit by the next flash of lightning, and I can tell by the set of her lips that, yes, she *was* torturing me.

There's not enough blood left in the rest of my body at this point. It's all painfully concentrated between my legs. There's still an entire room between us, but the hairs on the back of my arms stand up.

Something about the storm has freed Eva.

From what, I don't know.

From what, I don't care.

She turns around.

I hadn't turned on a lot of the lights in the main room in the first place—just a light over the stove and a little lamp with a cover meant to look like birch bark at the far end of the room.

Just as Eva's nipples—and holy *fuck* are they exquisite —come into view, the lights flicker once, twice, and then go out.

The storm rages and howls.

Eva glances downward.

It's one moment, one change, but that's all it takes. The confidence I saw a minute ago wasn't an illusion, but it ebbs and flows, and that flicker of her eyelashes might as well be an invitation. A wave needs a shore to crash into, is what I'm saying.

The room might as well be nothing. It might as well take me one step to cross it, because in the blink of an eye, I'm standing on the rug in front of Eva.

Lightning. Thunder.

And just like that, she's a fucking queen.

I sink down to my knees in front of her and hook my thumbs in the waistband of her panties. At the first touch, she gasps. I don't hear it; I see it in the way her stomach curves inward. It happens again and again with every inch that I tug the black athletic fabric down her thighs, over her knees, and to the floor.

I don't care what happens to them next.

All I care about is the shadowy cleft between Eva's legs. Another bolt of lightning casts everything in white light, and I don't need more than that split second to see her skin there is perfectly smooth.

I take her thighs in my hands and spread them apart. She helps me; she has to. Eva plants her feet against the rug and leans forward, bracing herself on my shoulders with trembling hands. Wider. *Wider.*

I spread her apart with the pads of my thumbs and she moans into my ear. This time, I hear it, and the sound snaps at something inside me.

I'm already breathing the sweet scent of her in and there's nothing—not water, not cloth, not light—to stop me from leaning forward and licking her like an open fruit.

So I do.

Eva's hands dig into my shoulders, her nails carving little crescents into my skin, and the rain on the roof drowns out the sound she makes, but it can't stop the vibration of it through her skin and bones. I feel it in my palms. I take another greedy lick, tasting her on my tongue. She's as sweet as I thought she'd be. Sweeter, even. I never would have joined the army if I knew a person could taste like this. I would have spent my life searching the country for her instead.

Never, never, never.

Her legs shudder in my hands, and when I suck her clit

into my mouth, the sound she makes mixes with the *boom* of the thunder through her body and I'm rewarded with another burst of her sweetness on my tongue.

The army gave me a lifetime's worth of questions. It gave me an unrelenting desire to find the answers. And it made me strong enough to survive the search. It made me tough. Too fucking tough. The only other relationship I had after I got out withered and died when I was walking across the desert with American money and cigarettes stuffed into my pockets.

I gave up everything to get the answers I was looking for.

But right now?

This is holy fucking communion.

This might be divine intervention.

I don't care about anything but my mouth on Eva's willing flesh and the taste of her on my tongue and my knees sinking into the rug beneath her feet.

The lightning cracks again.

I only need one more answer.

I dive deep, licking her like I'll never get another

chance, and then I stand up and sweep her into my arms. I can't hear anything over the rain, but I can feel the little sounds she's making. Like a prayer. Or maybe she's begging. Maybe it's both.

The bedroom is too far for what I want to do to her.

For what I *need* from her.

I go for the first blank stretch of wall like a man possessed. Her legs tighten around me when her back hits the paint, and with one hand, I reach down and shove my boxers out of the way.

A flash, and Eva is frozen in my memory this way, with her back arched against the wall, eyes closed, arms around my neck. She holds tight even though she doesn't have to. I wouldn't let her fall for the world.

I have to force us apart to get the leverage I need, to lower her down to the perfect angle, and even though we're still touching, it's a battle. She has nowhere to go, and I have nowhere else I want to be.

The next flash lights up Eva's eyes. She's looking at me, watching, and the expression on her face is like nothing I've seen before. There's no filter. There's only naked lust. Eva leans her head down next to my ear and says, *"Please, please, please."*

I drive into her in one stroke and she tips her head back against the wall. The sound that tears from her throat is pure pleasure, verging on pain, and I'm not surprised; she's tight and swollen from all my licking and sucking.

It doesn't make me want to slow down.

I can't slow down.

We have both been running nonstop for a long, long time, even when it looked like we were walking. She might as well have sprinted into that party at Whit and Wes's place. Maybe it seemed like I was casually sitting in the living room with some beer, but I fucking wasn't. I was on leave from a racing mind and a restless soul, and nothing on earth could stop it.

Until now.

She's light in my hands, light enough for me to rock her hips forward and pull her down onto me with every stroke. Her muscles tighten around me again and again. How can she get *tighter,* how can she be any slicker, and how can this be such a perfect fit?

It's enough to shatter my mind.

And it would, except I never want to forget a single moment of this. Even while the need builds, my balls tightening up between my legs, begging for release, I keep my eyes on Eva. I keep breathing her in. I keep reminding myself over and over of the way her skin is so soft and still so slick underneath my hands.

I'm going to come.

It's going to be hard and it's going to be rough and there's nothing I can do to stop it. All I can do is ride the wave.

And...reach forward to press my thumb against Eva's clit.

It sets her off like a firework. Her release is a gift and torture, because it makes it unbearable to exist without my own orgasm, which is exactly what I thought it would be when it comes—vicious, like I've been denying myself for too long.

I open my eyes.

I didn't know I'd shut them.

Eva tilts her head down to my lips, and between rolls of thunder when I can hear her, she says, "More."

THAT. Was. *Everything.*

I wake up early feeling like I slept all night, which in a way, I did, and in another way, I totally didn't. Bennett is still sleeping deeply on the other side of the bed. If he's as spent as I feel, he'll be asleep for a long time.

But I want to talk.

I pull on a sweatshirt and yoga pants and take my phone outside. The grass is covered in dew, but I don't care.

At all.

Whitney answers on the first ring.

"Eva! Oh my God. Are you okay? Where have you been? Are you still in the country?"

"Yes, did—did I miss plans we had?"

"You didn't miss them so much as showed up and bailed. You do remember my party, right? I am *worried* about you. I don't even care about the party. You looked...*pale* when you left with Bennett Powell." Whitney gasps. "Are you still *with* him?"

"Do I even need to be part of this conversation?"

Whitney laughs. "I feel like I'm missing most of the story."

"I told him about a problem I've been having. And he thought a getaway to this nice-as-hell cabin on a lake was the solution."

"How many bedrooms does it have?"

"Two," I say.

There's silence.

It stretches on.

"Eva, I swear to God—"

"We're only using one of them at present."

Whitney is glee personified. I don't have to be in the same room to see the grin on her face.

"The thing is—"

"Oh, what could *possibly* be wrong with Bennett Powell? Have you *looked* at him? Did he not whisk you away for a *getaway*?"

"The thing is, I'm not sure I can...or I should...be with him. Because then...." My throat gets all tight and weird.

"Because of the thing with your family?"

"We haven't really talked about it. I never talk about it, Whit. I barely ever mentioned it at school."

"You didn't have to mention it, obviously. Most of us were at the funeral. At least, I was. There were a bunch of us there."

This is news to me. All I remember is a blur of faces and hugs, because back then, I really was in shock. "You did? But we were just kids. How did you—"

"Girl, everyone's parents went. From the entire class. Some kids stayed home since we were young, but mine took me along. They didn't share, you know, the details, but...people talked. Anyway, I am not so confident in the rumors of children that I didn't confirm it for myself."

"There are.. other details."

"Eva." I can practically see her sitting up straight in the cubicle at her job, fixing her gaze on her Man of the Year pinup. "You don't have to tell him anything you don't want to. You don't have to tell *me* anything you don't want to." There's a pause. "But don't psych yourself out because the two of you don't know everything there is to know about each other yet. I'm sure there's plenty you don't know about him."

"Really?" I go closer to the sand and wiggle my toes in it. "He doesn't seem like the kind of guy who'd have a lot of secrets."

"Everyone has secrets," Eva intones. "To have secrets is but to be human, and to fear them is only to cloak them in darkness, which—"

"I get it." I laugh. "I really do."

"Do you?" There's a creak in the background, Whit leaning back in her chair. "Because you sound tense."

"I'm slightly tense. But I'm slightly—"

"You little minx," she says, and it makes me laugh, the

sound echoing over the water. "How long did you two —" Whit lowers her voice. "—*go at it* last night? Tell me it was hours. No! Tell me you've been up all night, and he's finally passed out. No! Tell me—"

"There was a thunderstorm," I offer. I don't really have the words to tell Whitney what happened. Well, I do, but there's no part of me that wants to say *Bennett Powell has the most perfect dick I've ever seen* and *he knows what he's doing with it.* That, and his hands. And his mouth....

"Hot," she says. "*Hot.*" Then: "Ms. Lipton, I assure you, we only offer the best when it comes to life insurance. Your family will be well taken care of if you decide to purchase a policy from us. We have our No Worry Guarantee, and.... Sorry, my boss just walked by."

"Go back to work! I just wanted to—"

"Chat with your very best friend. I get it. I get that way after Wes and I have a particularly—No, no. That guarantee *never* expires. You can trust it from now until the day your family needs to cash in on the policy."

"Love you, Whit."

"Love you too. Are you and Ben going to the meet-up this weekend?"

"Meet-up?"

"You know—for the Warriors?"

So maybe Ben *does* have more secrets than I thought. It intrigues me, and it makes me feel vaguely ill. Which... why? I've been keeping secrets from him too.

"He's in it with Wes," Whitney prompts. "There's a hangout this weekend. It's different from the usual Friday night meet-ups. Some private trivia night, and significant others are invited. On Saturday?"

"Oh, yeah, *right*. Right, that."

Whitney laughs. "So you two haven't talked about it."

"No. No, we haven't. But I would. I might go." I still don't want to go. Whitney's party was a disaster, but then there's the thought of being somewhere with Ben. And my guess is, a roomful of men like him wouldn't be the type to pry about my writing career. Even if he is a world-class pry-er.

"Lies," she says with a sigh. "What's going on with you, Eva?"

I open my mouth to tell her.

"Eva."

It's Ben's voice, low and gravelly from sleep.

"Is that him?" Whitney asks. "I heard something in the background. Is it time for round two? Or *wait.* Is this round three? Five? You don't have to tell me. But, really, tell me. *Six?*"

"I'll call you later," I tell her.

"Come back to bed," says Ben.

IT'S SLOWER THIS TIME, not so volatile and hard, and in the morning light, Ben takes his time exploring my body.

He spreads me open wide.

His eyes aren't on my face. They're between my legs.

"Does this embarrass you?"

"Does what embarrass me?"

"The way I'm looking at you."

He *is* looking at me. Like he wants to devour me...again. He has my legs spread open wide, thumbs moving in gentle, torturous circles on the insides of my thighs, and I honestly hadn't thought about it until he said something.

"In the light of day, yes. It's very bright in here," I whisper. I can feel all of me heating up. I wonder if he can see it between my legs. My guess is yes.

"And you love it."

I stretch my hands above my head. "I won't admit it."

"You don't have to." Ben sinks two fingers into me. There's hardly any resistance I'm so wet. "Your pussy gives you away."

I tighten around those fingers and he bends his head. The pressure and suck on my clit has every muscle vibrating with that pleasure, and he takes it slow, so slow.

"God, you're the worst."

He raises his mouth from my body and I let out a mewl that I have never heard myself make before. "What do you think now?" he asks.

"*This* is the worst. This. This. Please—"

"So pretty when you say that," Ben murmurs, and then he goes back to his work. The man is methodical, patient, and he's being *so* unkind as he brings me up to the very edge of release then backs off, rubbing at my clit with the pad of his thumb. I'm breathless with anticipation, my mind a haze of need and want and *oh fuck that feels good, yes, more of that, yes*. This is what we should have been doing all along. No massage, no glass of wine, could compare to this.

He makes me come with his tongue, bracing my legs apart with his arms, and I am so utterly exposed that it feels dirty, feels filthy, feels right. And then he makes me come on my hands and knees, ass in the air, with his fingers. When the shaking stops he takes my thighs in his hands and spreads them another inch apart and blows between my legs, the cool of his breath on the hot swollen skin making goose bumps rise on my arms.

And then...those fingers.

He takes another long, slow lick, my cheek pressed to the pillow and my back arched in a way that I honestly never thought it would be with another human, and I groan at how wrong and how good it feels. I have another little aftershock of an orgasm right then. His fingers never stop working my clit. He's figured out the exact degree of pressure I need, and he will not relent, he won't—

"How many times?" I gasp.

"How many times what?" Ben's voice is calm and languid, though I'd bet anything that he's hard as steel right now and biding his time.

"How many times are you going to make me come before you fuck me?"

I'm *never* this outspoken about it. I'm *never* this explicit. But I need him like I need air and light.

"Until you're a puddle." His breath is close to my ear. More goose bumps. "Until every single thought is chased from your mind. Until you're a clean slate. A white rose. Until nothing in the world worries you."

"But I can't..." Even while I'm protesting, I come again, this one slow and electric. "I can't keep... please, Ben, I need—"

"To be fucked?"

"I need to be fucked."

I feel the hard length of him against my entrance, and I arch my back a little farther, opening as much as I can. It's not how I normally am. It's not how anything normally is. But here, in this room, with Ben, I'm getting exactly what I want.

To hell with the consequences.

He pushes in another few inches. I'm sopping and swollen and I feel his groan right in the center of me. "That's good. That's so fucking good," he growls.

"Harder?"

"You'll take what you're given and you'll like it."

My nipples tighten at the words.

"Christ, you liked *that*," he says, his voice rough. "You got even wetter." His hands are still down between my legs, fingers still circling my clit. "I love how your face gets red when I tell you these things." Ben shoves in the rest of the way, our bodies obscenely connected. "Are you ashamed to be fucked?"

"No," I breathe.

His fingers press harder, and I'm on the precipice of a vicious release. This one's going to be the last one for at least until evening. It's brewing like last night's storm, and with Ben filling me so completely, there's no room for anything but heat and desire.

"Then what are you ashamed of?"

"You're going to make me come like this?"

"Yes. I'm going to make you come while you're impaled on my cock, totally exposed to me, totally under my control." He grips my hip, tugging me back against him. It's like a gate has slammed open, and I'm totally wanton. I *need* these words from him. I need him to tell me these dirty things, because—

"That's what I'm ashamed of." I get the words out through clenched teeth, because oh, when this one comes, it's going to be....

"Being fucked like this?"

"Being seen."

Another whisper, close to my ear, and I have never been so aware of how open I am, how every shift of the air against my skin is as thick as a sheet—

"I see you." Ben's voice is almost too low to compete with the ceiling fan. "And I'm not going to look away." His fingers, circling, circling, and the rock of his hips that pushes him in, and in, and in. "And here's the filthy truth, sweetheart."

I open my mouth to say *what*? And all that comes out is a moan.

"You say you're ashamed, but you love it. You fucking

love it. You're wetter than you've ever been, and I can feel *all* of it. I can see *all* of it."

Maybe he keeps talking. Maybe he stops. But all I know is that the wave of release breaks over me in an enormous jagged rush of pleasure that explodes outward from the core of me, all the way to my finger-tips. Is it me making that sound? It's definitely Ben pinning my hips in his hands while I rock and shudder and cry out. At some point, I can't tell when, he falls into his own release, fucking me with all the power he has in his body. My hands hit the headboard. I brace myself. I hold on.

And when it's over, I'm a puddle.

That means I have no fear of the consequences when I say, to his warm and breathing self with one arm thrown over my waist, "Tell me a secret, Ben. Just one."

14

IT PULLS a laugh right out of me. I've melted her mind. She's just deflecting. Eva must be an open book, ready to tell me anything, and some part of her—some animal part, deep down—is fighting it.

"I don't have any secrets."

She opens her green eyes and pushes herself up on one elbow. "We both know that's not true."

I give her a look. "Are you secretly in the CIA? Because if you are, you should tell me." I narrow my eyes. "Or maybe...you can't."

Eva is flushed and pink, eyes shining. "I talked to Whitney this morning."

"Oh, yeah? What does Whitney have to say about me?"

Eva reaches out and walks her fingers all the way down my abs to a spot that's dangerously south. "She mentioned a certain...crowd that you're part of."

I have no earthly idea what she's talking about.

"A...group," Eva prompts. "That you didn't ever tell me about."

Oh. *Oh.* "Wow. I can't believe she revealed the secret of my *veterans support group.* Which is not a secret at all."

"You didn't say anything about it though."

"When would I have slipped that in? In the middle of fucking you? '*Oh, by the way, twice a month I hang out with a group of vets and we call ourselves the Warriors'?*"

"You have a name for your group?" Eva's eyes are wide.

"Would *you* want to reserve a room under the name Veterans Support Group? It sounds...sad."

"It does, kind of," she admits. "But why didn't you tell me about the meet-up?"

"You're going to have to help me out here. What meet-up are you talking about? Hey." I narrow my eyes. "Are *you* in the support group? Is that how you have all this insider information?"

Eva rolls her eyes. "No. Obviously, Wes is in the support group. You know. Wes. Your friend. For an undisclosed amount of time...."

"Since we were in the army together."

She flicks her gaze downward. "Just at the same time, or...?"

"We were in the same unit. We were deployed togeth-er." The hairs on the back of my neck rise. "Has Whitney ever told you about what happened to Wes in Afghanistan?"

"Some of it," Eva says. "An IED and a Humvee. I guess it got to him after a while."

"It got to all of us. In different ways."

"Everyone in the unit?"

"Everyone in the Humvee."

Eva's green eyes fly back to mine. "I knew you were in the Humvee. I didn't know it...got to you like that."

"I'm surprised she didn't tell you."

"We've spent far more time discussing her love life." Eva raises her eyebrows, a little color coming to her cheeks. Whitney must have described some pretty wild things if Eva is embarrassed after what we just did.

I resist the urge to change the topic entirely. What happened in the Humvee was something that took over my life for the better part of eighteen months, and that's not a story I relish going over with her. Not today, and maybe not ever. At any rate, I've put it to bed.

I can tell Eva's waiting to hear more about it, but she just traces the lines of my abs with a fingertip. So casual. So patient.

"I was in the Humvee," I confirm. "On the day it hit the IED."

"But you weren't hurt."

"No, but that kind of shit will shake you to your core. The explosion was one thing. Seeing my buddies...."

"Dayton."

"Yeah. He was pretty torn up."

I keep these memories at bay, where they can't touch

me, but even at a distance, they're still not the kinds of things I want to think about. The sound Dayton made. The way Wes rushed straight out of the Humvee and around to the other side. Really, the silence was worse, once Dayton stopped making any noise at all.

"It was one of those moments."

"Yeah," Eva says, as if she understands perfectly.

I watch the sun play over her hair for a long moment. She looks back up at me, that same light catching in her eyes, and I forget all of it. Afghanistan. The Humvee. The year and a half I spent chasing answers about it.

And I forget it still isn't enough.

Eva lifts her hand to my face, and now it's her turn to watch me.

Are the questions I see in her eyes about me, or about something else entirely?

I'll answer her, if that's what I want.

But I can smell them in the air around us—her secrets. They're so close to the surface. I've given up one of mine—low-stakes, that's true—but I could ask. I could find out. I could—

"I'm starving," says Eva. "Let's make lunch."

I SIT her at the counter and put her laptop in front of her.

"Here's the deal."

"Oh?" She gives me a coy smile. "Are we dealing again? Is this another contest?"

"No, it's actually a deal." I pull out a frying pan from the cupboards beneath the kitchen island, where she sits on a high-backed stool. "You write, I cook."

Eva screws up her lips. "This sounds like I won't get to eat if I don't write."

I brandish a spatula in her general direction. "You're absolutely right."

She puts her hands dutifully on the keyboard, but I feel her eyes on my back the moment I turn around and start going through the fridge. I had the owners stock it before we came, so there's plenty here to make meals. I have a feeling we'll be cooking everything in here, after the near miss with the semi yesterday.

I get three bell peppers out of the crisper, locate a cutting board, and prepare them for slaughter. Eva watches me cut through them. I add a little oil to the frying pan and toss in the peppers. An onion is next.

"I don't hear typing," I tell her.

"Where did you learn to cook?" Eva's big green eyes follow me as I pull out a second pan, melt some butter into it, and produce a package of chicken breasts from the fridge, plus another cutting board.

"We didn't have a ton of money growing up." I slice the chicken into strips, cutting away all the weird pieces. Maybe Eva doesn't mind the weird bits in chicken, but I sure as hell do. "So my dad taught me to cook."

"Your dad?" She's tentative, which is cute.

"Yeah, my mom wasn't around."

I see Eva's frown out of the corner of my eye. "I'm sorry to hear that."

"Don't be." I flash her a quick grin, and she smiles back. "She took off when I was three. It was a middle-of-the-night escape. For years, my dad told me that she'd left to find a better job and send money back to the two of us. It was bullshit."

"Where'd she go then?"

"Who knows?" Somewhere, distantly, it still hurts, like

an old stab wound that's never healed. But I'm not going to let myself get sucked in to that pain. It would be pointless, and it would be poison. "She never sent any money back. My dad was too proud to take her to court over it, so...." I dump the chicken into the frying pan. I'll brown it on both sides then add it to the veggies. "Eventually, some stuff with bank accounts made it necessary to have her declared dead. She might be dead. I don't know. I don't really care at this point." I wash my hands in the sink and glance back to Eva.

"You seriously don't care? You're not curious about it?" she asks. "That seems unlike you."

"There are other things I'm more curious about. Things that meant more to me over the course of my life than that woman ever did."

"Like what?" Eva, for all her insistence on keeping everything tamped down, is practically glowing at the thought of learning more about me.

I wield the spatula again, pointing it at her. "You are subverting the rules. The deal is food for words. And you know that means *written* words, not spoken ones."

She purses her lips. "You'd really punish me if I didn't get enough work done?"

My cock is instantly at attention. I've never been much for the BDSM scene, but you can be sure as hell that I'd put Eva over my knees if that's how she's going to tease. Honestly, her ass might have caused a new awakening in my soul. I want to see it in every possible position, and right now, I wouldn't mind putting a few handprints—

Eva laughs. "Did I say the wrong thing? I feel like you're looking way beneath my skin."

I narrow my eyes at her. "Don't tempt me with punishment." The smell of the frying veggies and the chicken waft into the air. "Because if you want to play those games, we're not going to get *anything* done."

I reach for the cabinet above the stove and pull out some Mrs. Dash spice. My dad always used the original kind, so I use the original kind. Exploration is one thing, but when it comes to chicken, there's no need to reinvent the wheel.

The dulcet tones of Eva's keyboard mix in with the crackle and pop from the frying pans. I nudge everything around in the pots with the spatula then turn around to survey my handiwork.

With a face as red as a tomato, Eva's typing, her eyes glued to the screen. She's shifting a little in her seat, which leads me to believe she's pressing her thighs against one another.

I lean on the counter and look across at her until she meets my eyes.

"It's not fair, you know. You already finished all your work."

"That's not true. I have another job." The moment the words are out of my mouth, I regret it. This is the getaway of a lifetime with a girl like Eva. I don't want to ruin it by getting into all my obsessions.

But she lets the comment slide right on by. "Still." She taps out a few more words on the keyboard. I'm tempted to go around and see if it's gibberish, but I won't. This is the first thing she's typed besides **Chapter One** since we got here.

"Hey, Eva?"

"Yeah?"

"Are you writing the world's sexiest psychological thriller?"

She gives me a little smile. "Maybe."

"Is that why your face is so red?" I lean in closer. "Or

do you relish the thought of being punished by yours truly?"

Eva laughs out loud. "Look, we're straying into weird territory. Territory that's too inappropriate for a writer's retreat."

I cock my head to the side. "Is there always so much sex at a writer's retreat?"

"I wouldn't know." Eva's blush somehow reaches a deeper shade of red. "I've never been on one before."

"You're a famous writer and you've never been on a writer's retreat?"

"You're a famous fact-checker," she shoots back. "Haven't you ever been on a fact-checking retreat?"

"Are a lot of other fact-checkers in the market for a rustic getaway far from the Internet?" That would be some hilarious shit.

"I wouldn't know," Eva says primly.

"I can tell you this much. There's no such thing as a retreat from my job. The only way to get any deeper into it is to go on-site."

"Like traveling?"

"Like traveling."

"For articles? That seems expensive. You know. Publishing-wise."

"I usually don't travel for my paid work." There it is. Out in the open. She can't miss it now. And in the light of day...it does matter. In the light of day, I know I can't give it up. Not for good.

"What kind of fact-checker does unpaid work?" Eva wrinkles her nose. "That seems like it would be—"

"We had a *deal*." I flip the veggies in the frying pan one more time, the colors flying up into the air and back down. "Words for food."

"I want food *and* words." She puts her hands flat on the keyboard. "I want to know more of your secrets, Ben."

"Be careful what you wish for, sweetheart."

Eva laughs. She's right; it was an incredible joke.

15

I'VE NEVER BEEN hungrier in my life.

"I am careful with what I wish for," I say quietly, but Bennett turns back to his work with a smirk that makes me feel like melting into a sexual puddle.

I focus on the screen, letting the pure white of the empty Word document envelop me like a blanket of clean snow. It is not my antagonist. We simply exist in the world together.

The food smells...wholesome. Normal. Good. It's not takeout, saturated with fat and sugar and God knows what else, and it doesn't smell like the shame of another box of Kraft Macaroni and Cheese. Not that I have anything against Kraft Macaroni and Cheese. It's just the thing that I tend to eat when I'm in panic-writing-avoidance mode.

Ask me how I know they sell 15-packs of Kraft Macaroni and Cheese at Costco.

The other upside to this little venture is that Bennett looks unbelievably hot standing there in the kitchen in his T-shirt. It's your average, run-of-the-mill gray T-shirt, but it might as well cost a million dollars for how it accentuates his biceps.

Plus, that fabric is all that's protecting his once-in-a-lifetime abs from the ravages of the outside world.

For the first time in a long time, nothing else seems to matter aside from this counter and this man. We're safe behind the walls of this cabin. It's like they're imbued with a magical force field that keeps the pressure of my editing deadline and the larger guillotine of my publishing contract at bay.

The young woman in the backpack comes back to me.

She needs money; that's her first thought, and there she is, sprung to life on the page. Something from nothing.

She needs money... but why?

The college she attends sprouts from the ground

around her, a Midwestern university collection of old ivy-covered buildings tucked around boxy monstrosities from the sixties.

Money doesn't always have to be tangible. It's not crumpled bills shoved into her pockets, though she could use that too. What she needs is a roommate.

The situation she's coming from in this moment plays out in fast-forward in front of my eyes. I won't put it on the page, not in all its humiliating details—not now, not yet. I'll hold it in reserve. What's important is that I know about it. I know about the bitchy middle-aged woman in the financial aid office telling my heroine that nobody is going to give her a loan for room and board, especially not the university. Not this late in the process, and maybe not ever.

Which explains why my heroine is more desperate than ever, hustling across campus in a late August storm, hair dripping wet.

She has one last shred of hope for this day.

And that hope is to find a roommate.

The listing on RoommateNow.com seems too good to be true, but now that there's no chance of living in the dorms, she's out of options. And she doesn't want to stay in the seedy weekly motel she's been living in. I leave a note to myself midway through the paragraph around the hotel that something else happened to this heroine to put her in the hotel in the first place. It's on the very edge of my mind, and I'll flesh it out later. I'll come back to it.

I have to keep this momentum going.

The house she arrives at is an old Victorian. In the rain, it looks haunted. **Haunted as fuck,** I write, which is surprising, because I normally don't write *"as fuck"* anything, but I won't muzzle my muse. I can finesse that description later.

The girl who enters the door looks like another student in the best kind of way. Preppy. Clean. Dark hair that falls in a shining sheet to her shoulders. They could be friends, or at least cordial. She ushers her back into the kitchen and gives her a dishtowel to dry her hair. The dishtowel appears clean at first glance, but the heroine thinks she sees the ghost of a stain on it. That's not weird, is it?

It must be the weather, the stress of the financial aid office, getting her down.

The other student is running through the details of the house. They'll share the main floor. The home is owned by an old woman named Gladys, who lives on the upper floor. All utilities are included in the rent. They just need to be there in order to keep up the house, though Gladys hires a couple of different services that come in for lawn mowing and sidewalk shoveling. The responsibilities are minor and the first floor of the house is nice. When can she move in?

The heroine is surprised.

She hasn't said very much. She's laughed a few times and leaned against the kitchen island and sipped some hot cocoa, and now this other student wants *her* to live in the house?

She remembers the motel, and the way the couple three rooms down screams at each other all night. And how afraid she is that the deadbolt won't keep anything out, not with such a flimsy door.

She agrees to move in. She'll be there tomorrow, she tells her new roommate. Desperate isn't a good look on anybody, so she'll live one more night in the motel.

The next day, what will she do?

She'll go to school. In her first class of the day, she'll meet a chatty new friend, Elizabeth. Elizabeth will ask her which dorm she's living in, and for some reason, she won't lie. Elizabeth will frown at the address she names. "What?" she'll ask. "Have you heard something weird about it?"

Elizabeth's face will brighten. "No, it must be a different place. You know how places are in the city. One bad year of renters and everybody thinks they're cursed. Do you have plans for between classes? I'm dying for a latte."

With the stress of finding a place to stay lifted from her shoulders, my heroine has become...approachable.

Usually, she works every spare second, but today the stars align. Today, she has no mini shift between classes. She can go for a latte with her new friend. Well, not a latte. Whatever the smallest, cheapest black coffee is.

Her name is Chloe.

That's what she'll tell the barista, my heroine.

That's the name she'll give when she orders the coffee.

Chloe will run into her new roommate on the way out of the coffee shop, and that gorgeous dark-haired girl will be surprised to see her. "You're here? What are you doing out here?"

Chloe will lift the coffee, feeling the eyes of Elizabeth her classmate ping-ponging between the two of them. "Coffee," she'll say tentatively. "Before my next class."

The new roommate narrows her eyes and then, without another word, moves past them into the coffee shop.

"What the hell was that?" Elizabeth says, laughing.

"My new roommate," Chloe tells her.

"Maybe I had the right idea about that house after all."

Yes. *Yes.* That's creepy. That's foreboding. That's a damn good start. And that's—

That's a thousand words.

I surface from the page like I'm coming up from deep water, and when my head breaks the surface I can tell by the light coming in from the kitchen window that time has passed, but how much? I have an app on my computer that blanks out all the clocks so it doesn't stress me. Obviously, none of that was working until now.

Ben leans against the counter by the kitchen sink. His eyes catch mine across the space and he grins then lifts a final forkful from his plate to his lips. Then he lets the plate fall into the sink with a clatter.

"You started without me?"

"Do you think for an instant I was going to interrupt you? You were in the *zone,* Eva."

My stomach growls and I have a more pressing concern. "Is the food cold?"

Ben laughs then turns to the microwave tucked into the corner of the counter. "I've been reheating it every five minutes."

"Every five minutes since when?"

"For the last hour."

I blink at him.

"It's slightly creepy to stand there and watch someone writing for an hour."

He takes a full plate out of the microwave and opens one of the kitchen drawers. It's only when he turns that he responds to what I've said. "You know I like to look at you."

See, I'm *pretty* sure my face had returned to its normal

color. Eight words from Bennett Powell, and it might as well be on fire again.

"But I didn't stand here for an hour. I ate my first plate—" He reaches out, nudges my laptop aside, and puts the plate in front of me, following it up with a fork and a napkin. "—and then I went and worked outside. You must have really been in it if you didn't hear me coming in and out to tend to the food this entire time."

"I *was* in it," I admit while I pick up my fork.

I say it casually. As if being "in it" has come naturally to me for the last...forever. The words slip out of my mouth like it's no big deal. Like I have been talking to Bennett Powell about having a good writing hour for all my life.

"You were," he says.

"I was...*in it*."

He's an angel descended from heaven, because he didn't actually close my laptop when he moved it; he just pushed it aside. It's like he can see right through me into my secret fears. One of those fears is that if I close my laptop before I've hit *save* on a document, it will disappear before I can get the screen back open.

And before you think I'm paranoid, this has happened to me more than once.

Wait.

I reach over to the laptop keyboard with my left hand and delicately, *so* delicately, scroll up to the top of the page.

"I was in it," I whisper to myself.

It's a little rusty, for sure. There are things that Kayla's going to mark for rewrites—I absolutely know it. And it was pretty slow going. Usually, when I have a solid grasp on an idea, I can write two thousand words in an hour, maybe even more. When my heart is pounding and the horrible twist is about to be revealed, there's no telling how fast I can get those words out onto the page.

"I was in it!" I shout, throwing my arms into the air.

"Damn right you were," Bennett shouts back.

I wheel on him. "*You.*" I jab a finger at him. "This is because of *you.*"

He raises his eyebrows at me. "Is this a bad thing? I was under the impression that—"

It takes me four huge steps to get around the kitchen counter to where Bennett is standing. He looks down at me with those steady brown eyes, starlight shot through them, and there's that smirk again.

"Don't you dare smirk at me," I challenge.

"I think you were in the middle of complimenting me. Or better yet, *thanking* me. Profusely."

"It's black magic," I say. I feel drunk on the fact that I just got a thousand words on paper and it didn't hurt. I didn't feel breathless and stupid and incapable. "How did you... how did you get that to happen?"

Ben crosses his arms over his chest and arranges his face into something resembling a serious adult expression. "I cooked chicken. You seem to respond very well to rewards involving chicken." He cocks his head to the side. "Or maybe you were responding to the threat of punishment."

I swallow hard.

"But you're the one who made it happen, Eva. You could do it again and again until your book is done."

My fists shoot out from my body as if they're not under my own control, and then I've got the tightest grip of my life on the front of his T-shirt. "I don't care about the secrets." My heart beats a rabbit-fast rhythm in my chest.

Ben hasn't moved. "What?"

"I don't care if you tell me any secrets. But you *cannot* bail on me. Do you understand?" Maybe it's pathetic of me. Maybe it's weak. But I don't care. We're in this magical getaway cabin, and I'm going to say it out loud, even if I'm out of practice. Even if I'd normally cover this up and forget about it. "I need your rewards." My breath catches. "Or your punishments."

Ben's eyes are hot coals burning into mine. "All of it's yours."

"Yeah?"

"If you can wait fifteen more minutes to eat."

"I can wait a year. Try me."

16

Eva tips her head back, exposing the long line of her throat, and I take advantage of her little moans to roll her peaked nipples between my fingers. She bites her lip, her eyebrows drawing together.

We're outside in the larger of the two lawn chairs. I am a cruel taskmaster, so I'm fully clothed, but Eva is down to a neon pink pair of panties.

She rocks her hips forward but can't get anywhere. Not in my grip. I'm holding her too tight to let her rub on the front of my shorts, and it only takes one hand. She knows the game we're playing.

I dip my other hand between her legs and drag my fingers along the damp fabric.

The moan turns into a groan. "Come on, Ben. Come on...."

I lean forward so my mouth is next to her ear. "It's another thousand words if you want these panties off."

Eva snaps her head up, green eyes blazing, and fixes me with a stare that could melt steel. "You're mean."

"You love it."

There's a moment of shyness, a little bit of that wall coming back up, and Eva pouts. "I need it."

"Nothing wrong with needing a little incentive to get your work done." I trace the curve of her chin with my finger and tilt her face back to mine.

"But what am I going to do when—"

"Shh." I press that same finger against her lips. "No questions about the future on our magical sex writer's retreat."

Eva laughs and the movement makes me even harder. I'm not only teasing her. My own cock wants to know what made me such an asshole. "Even if it's about the immediate future?"

"What immediate future?"

"It's Wednesday." Eva hooks a finger in the neckline of my T-shirt and tugs lightly at it, enough so that I feel the fabric drawing closer on my back. "The meet-up is this Saturday."

"You're still thinking about that? Why is that still on your mind?"

Eva looks out over the lake. We woke up early this morning, and as soon as we'd finished having our way with each other, I kicked her out of bed and made her write for her breakfast.

I love how she blushes when I set the terms.

"I feel bad about bailing on Whit's party like that. I could make up for it at the trivia night."

I take a fistful of Eva's hair in my hand and twist it gently in my palm. "Do you think you'll be done with your book by then?"

She gapes at me. "By *Saturday?*"

"By at least Saturday at noon. If you don't want to rush getting out of here."

"I don't want to rush it, but..."

There it is. That look in her eyes that plants cold doubt in my gut. I'd let myself feel it if Eva wasn't so warm and sitting in my lap.

"I probably won't be done by then," she admits. "And at some point, I have to go back to the city."

"For what?"

Her eyes graze over mine and then she looks back out at the water. "This isn't real life."

"Mmmm." I reach down between her spread legs and press one knuckle against her clit. Eva gasps as if I've touched a livewire. It doesn't seem to matter that she still has her panties on. "Did that feel real, or fake?"

Her back arches and she puts her palms flat on the arms of the lawn chair. "I don't.... You know, it seemed pretty fake to me." She presses toward my hand, a shift of an inch. "Maybe if you—"

I stand up, lifting us both from the chair, and set her on her feet. "A thousand more words, and I'll show you if it's real or not."

A THOUSAND WORDS FOR BREAKFAST. A thousand words for an orgasm. A thousand words to go out and write on the beach. Another thousand for me to fuck her underneath one of the oversized beach towels from the house. I charge two thousand to fuck her with no beach towel. *That,* Eva admits, *is real.* It's a miracle we don't get arrested. We would have been, if this cabin were on the fancy side of the lake.

At some point in the afternoon, I lose her.

Eva stops counting the words.

She digs a notebook out of her bag and perches at the kitchen counter, scribbling things into it. Every so often, she stops and types furiously.

I wait long enough to be sure she won't need me right away and then, finally, I let my mind go back to my own work.

I'm in the early phases of a fact-checking project for my job, but this phase is the lightest, with the team sending me snippets of draft material to check. All of it will be double and triple-checked. The nature of the work leaves a gap in my schedule.

I need the gap. I have a new lead.

The genealogy websites online can tell you a lot about your family tree, which is pertinent information for me. I need to know as much about my father as possible, and secondary sources are a way to do that.

But those websites only work when people enter their information. My father didn't do this, so all my searching came to nothing. Until I hired a woman out of New York, Robin, to tell me something I didn't already know.

Her email this morning was a bombshell.

Your father was adopted out of the foster system, she wrote. **He was a rare late adoptee at fourteen years old.**

The new knowledge is so strange it hurts to hold it inside my skin. My dad's adopted parents—it seems terrible to think of them that way—were busy people. They were affectionate when they could be, but they both worked at the Ford plant in Flat Rock and we lived up north in a nowhere town by a lake sort of like this one. It was a long drive for a day off, so we mostly saw them on holidays.

And nobody ever mentioned this.

Not one time.

I can't distract Eva with this. She's doing too well with her book to make that kind of rookie mistake.

But I can do something else.

His original last name was Siverling.

It seems odd to me, that name. It probably seems doubly odd, because if things had gone very differently in my father's life, it would have been my last name too.

No. I wouldn't have existed. If everything hadn't gone exactly the way it went, I wouldn't be sitting here in this lawn chair right now, tapping my father's secret into a search engine.

The results are slim. Too slim. One page of results on a Google search. I straighten my back. If Robin was wrong, then she was wrong. I can keep looking elsewhere. But it's possible this family didn't interface with the Internet very often.

I click on the third link down, which looks most promising. It's the genealogical profile of a man named Robert Siverling.

This could be my dad's dad.

The birthdays make sense for that.

I take out my phone and copy some of the information into a note. It looks like one of the Siverling daughters got interested in genealogy a few years ago and added in as much as she could. By the dates, the two girls in the family were much younger than my father. Old enough to have existed by the time he left—and how did he leave? Why? What the hell? But....

It's such an afterthought that I almost miss it. It's not even in the family tree section of the page; it's down below, in miscellaneous notes.

All it says is *H? 1961?*

I don't usually get emotional about this kind of thing. I saw enough in Afghanistan to know that getting yourself worked up over what's already said and done is a fool's errand. But it makes my throat tight to see this little note, never updated.

My father was part of another family.

And these people don't know that he's dead.

"DID YOU CHECK ALL THE FACTS?"

Eva's voice comes from behind me, from the front door of the cabin, and then the door closes and I hear her soft footsteps on the grass.

She comes into view next to me, wearing an oversized hoodie with holes in the sleeves where her thumbs can go. I take the hem of it in my fingers and tug her closer. "Who said you could put this on?"

"I got cold," she says haughtily. "I can't write when I'm too cold."

I pull her into my lap and we look out at the water together. The sun is beginning to set, orange and pink streaks across the surface. For a moment, it's enough to sit here with her, taking it in.

Then Eva turns to look at me. "You're not keeping up your end of the deal."

I exaggerate my shock. "What could you possibly be talking about? I have tended to you for *days*. I have motivated you, and—"

"I'm *very* motivated." She runs a hand over the side of my face, tracing the line of my jaw. "But you were supposed to start telling me secrets."

"We were both supposed to tell each other secrets."

Eva's eyes flick to the left then back to my face. "I don't have any secrets."

"Here's one: you're a terrible liar."

"Here's another: you're keeping secrets too. I want to know what your real job is."

"My real job?" I brush an auburn curl away from her face.

"There's no way a fact-checker can afford to take a sudden weeklong vacation and barely work."

"I work from home." I'm not sure where she's going with this. "I've always worked from home. Or, in this case, cabin."

"But you have time all day to cook from me. And tease me. And drive me crazy." She gives a little sigh. "Ben, if you're a secret trust fund baby, just tell me. You don't have to pretend to work."

"I'm not pretending to work." I narrow my eyes. "Are *you* pretending to work?"

"Hell no!" Eva shouts, and it makes me laugh. But she's serious. "I'm not faking this. This is really working. It's working so well that...that I don't know what I'll do without it."

I study the curves of her cheeks, the lines of her face. "Then why do you look like you're about to attend someone's funeral? Shouldn't that be a good thing?"

"Maybe not for you."

"See?" I pull her face toward mine and kiss her.

"You're the cryptic one. I'd bet my dinner you're not going to tell me what that means."

Eva presses her lips together. "I'm willing to make a deal."

"I like the deal we already have."

"You *would.*"

"What does *that* mean? Should we check and see how much you like it?" I reach between her legs, but she bats me away.

"Throw me a bone, Bennett Powell. Are you really and truly a fact-checker?"

I can't deny her. "Yes. You saw my dashboard. But I can't show you the individual projects, because my company contracts with government agencies."

Eva's mouth drops open. "You're a military Internet spy?"

"No." I laugh out loud. "I'm a fact-checker who used to be in the military. There's nothing James Bond about it. We're in a little bit of a lull right now while another project ramps up, which gives me more free time to spend with you."

"Were you getting ahead, then?"

"Getting ahead?"

"I saw you out here, you know. You're sitting in front of an open window, and you were working hard all afternoon."

Sooner or later, I'm going to have to tell her.

Sooner or later, we're going to have to face this.

"I'll tell you more."

Eva waits.

"For another thousand—"

She jumps up from the chair with a frustrated shriek and storms for the cabin. "Fine," she calls over her shoulder. "Be that way."

"Be a famous writer," I call back.

Eva pauses. "Fine."

Then the door slams behind her.

17

EVA

I can't sleep.

Being with Bennett Powell has turned my mind on again. I'm not sure exactly when it happened—if there was a single moment when he flipped the switch—but now I can't turn it off.

This book is starting to infiltrate everything. *Ben* is starting to infiltrate everything, if I'm being honest with myself.

After he fell asleep, I lay in bed staring at the ceiling fan whipping its blades, up there in the dark. I didn't want to be the asshole who tugs at the blankets and makes the bed shift from side to side all night, so I turned over carefully. Left side. Right side. On my back again, considering the fan. The cabin has central air, so a fan isn't strictly necessary, but the low hum of it is a comforting sound in the night. It didn't matter. Ceiling fan or not, nothing felt good enough to lull me off to dreamland.

So I got up as quietly as I could, tugged on a pair of leggings and a hoodie, and came out here, into the moonlight.

The story wends its way through my mind, the little tendrils of action and reaction growing like vines. I can see them now, the throughways into the next chapters. They get clearer all the time, like a ship drawing close to shore out of the fog.

I should use that metaphor in my book. It's a good one.

I think of that ship, and then my main character, Chloe, and all the trouble she's in.

There's a blanket on the couch in the cabin, and I sneak back inside and get it. All quiet on the cabin front, no hint of movement from the bedroom. Ben has got to be down for the count. He leaves it all on the field when we have sex. It's the kind of single-minded focus I would definitely highlight if I were putting him in a romance novel. Or, really, any novel. Who says thrillers can't have a romance in them?

All of my heroes would turn out to be just like Ben.

The heroines, on the other hand, they probably wouldn't be like me. They wouldn't harbor a secret fear that their new sexy cabin-mate might discover the very worst parts of them.

Or maybe they would.

An idea for a spinoff novel begins to form, and it feels like a sip of warm hot chocolate. Not the idea itself. Thrillers aren't supposed to be comforting like that. But just *having* an idea still seems like a small miracle.

I wrap the blanket around my shoulders and try one more time to convince myself that I'm tired enough to sleep.

It's not to be.

The lawn chair in the center of the lawn seems like the place to be. One of those outdoor swings would be even better, but you can't have everything.

The moonlight is concentrated in a pale ripple out in the center of the lake, and watching it is the kind of meditation I don't get from my app. My fingers itch to keep typing, and watching those little waves cools that itch. I know it's not going to last forever—the creative energy, I mean. I know it will get hard again.

I have to ride the wave now, while it's still cresting. Once I'm done out here, I'll go back in and work for an hour. I can always sleep late if my mind will settle.

The breeze kicks up, rustling across the shoreline and the sand and the grass, smelling like summer. There are so many stars visible at this place. It's nothing like the city, with its light pollution and its constant noise.

Not that nighttime by the lake is quiet, exactly. There's the gentle lap of water against the sand. Crickets and frogs sing in their relentless rhythm. The night is as close as the blanket around my shoulders.

It reminds me of another night like this one.

How old could I have been? Not very old. Five? Six? Old enough to know that I didn't particularly want to sleep in our family's pop-up camper. It smelled old and slightly musty, and the padding on the sleeping platform was worn in places. I don't think we even used it much. But the time I'm remembering was a family reunion.

It was my mom's family. She didn't have any siblings, but she had lots of aunts and uncles. They all seemed uniformly old to me, but they were nice enough. One of them—I think her name was Kathy—would sit in a folding chair by the water while I splashed in the shallows for hours.

So I should have been tired enough to sleep in the pop-up. But I hadn't been. I was too hyped-up, too drunk on the adrenaline of being with so many people all day, listening to so many voices.

My parents weren't paying much attention to me. After the big dinner that night, they hadn't noticed the pop I'd snuck or the half-bag of marshmallows. My mom hurried to put me to bed that night. She didn't stay to make sure I fell asleep.

That was how it went at those things. The adults sat around the campfire into the wee hours of the morning, talking about all sorts of bullshit that a six-year-old wouldn't care about. Still, their voices drew me in. I'd perched on the bench of a little picnic table outside the ring of light, wrapped in my sleeping bag, and listened.

My sister *loved* the pop-up.

Of course she did.

She was perfect.

She loved camping, and she loved being a part of that adult conversation. Emily sat next to my mom in a kid-sized folding chair, wearing one of my dad's hoodies. I thought she looked so cool. I though I could never be the one to sit there, up late, because I never had anything on her level to say. She was only two years older than me, but she might as well have been thirty. That's the way I saw her then.

But it wasn't what Emily did or said around the camp-fire that burrowed its way into my memory. She didn't do much of anything, aside from sit there. She must have been listening.

No, it was what my *mother* said that I never forgot.

The screen door creaks behind me.

"There you are. I woke up and you were gone." Ben's voice is low and gravelly with sleep. Plastic scrapes on brick, and a moment later, he comes into view next to me, dragging the other lawn chair. He plants it next to mine and sits down in it, stretching his arms over his head. "Are you okay?"

"I couldn't sleep."

He tilts his head back against the chair and looks up at the stars. I follow his gaze until I catch him looking back at me. There's just enough moonlight to tell. "Story on your mind?"

"It was." The breeze whispers through the leaves on the trees.

"That's good. Are you still working on the plot? Or did it get its claws in you?"

Somewhere in the distance, wind chimes ring, low and mournful. "I was. My mind moved on to other things."

"You can't tease me like that." Ben clears his throat. "What other things?"

I wait for the anxiety to come back. I've spent so much time the last few months drowning in a sea of it that the thought of telling Ben my unfiltered thoughts should bring it raging back, but it doesn't. Maybe the cover of darkness is my sweet spot.

"A memory. From a camping trip I took with my family when I was a kid."

He sits up straight and pushes his hands into the pocket of the sweatshirt he's wearing. "My dad used to take me on camping trips after we were solo. What were you remembering?"

It was warmer that night, almost too warm to sleep. Or maybe it only seemed that way because of the camp-fire. And afterward, my cheeks burned so hot I stayed awake until the light began to leach into the sky. I wait for the warning to sound in the back of my mind, telling me that I shouldn't get into this with Ben, but it's so muted by the water and the stars that I just talk over it.

"We used to go to these family reunions. Our house was usually quiet, but this kind of weekend was loud."

"And drunk?"

"Hell yes, the adults were drunk." This earns me a laugh from Ben. "Buzzed, really, because I think that's the only way to enjoy a family reunion. But I wasn't."

He pretends to be shocked. "You weren't a teenage lush?"

"At this one, I was only five or six, so no on both counts."

"You wouldn't have taken the risk anyway. Too much of a people-pleaser." Ben shakes his head. "You were probably one of those insufferably perfect kids."

He's kidding, but there's a little stab of pain. "No, that was my sister."

"At the camping trip?"

"Always." I take a deep breath and let it out. "The trip was at a cabin kind of like this one, by a lake. My mom was an only child *and* an only niece, so nobody else had any kids with them. It was my parents, me, my sister, and my mom's aunts and uncles."

"Old people."

"They seemed ancient. But some of them were nice."

"If they were so nice, what happened?"

I pull the blanket tighter around my shoulders. "What makes you so sure something happened?"

"The look on your face."

I give Ben an exaggerated smile that must look hideously creepy in the dark, and he laughs.

And then he waits.

"I was supposed to be sleeping."

Ben runs a hand over his face.

"We were staying in this pop-up camper. Did you ever have one of those?"

"My dad had a tent he bought right after he got out of the army."

"Maybe I would have liked a tent better." I think about it for a hot second and decide—no. I would not have liked to be so close to the ground. "Anyway, I was supposed to be sleeping in our pop-up, but like I said, there was enough beer to go around and nobody was really paying attention to what I was doing."

"And you got up to no good? I don't believe it."

"Yes. I did the incredibly risky thing of sitting at a picnic table in the yard."

"My God." Ben shakes his head. "Maybe I don't know anything about you, Eva. You're a daredevil."

Suddenly, the story is like water beating against a levee. If I could just get it out of me and into the night, I could leave it behind at this cabin.

"Yeah, I—" My voice catches, and I can feel the shift in the air between us. Ben leans forward, as close as he can get to me, and takes my hand.

"I'm sorry, Eva. I shouldn't have been joking."

Anger flares like an errant firework. "It was what she *said* that was such a disaster."

"Who?"

"My mother."

18

BENNETT

THE WAY EVA SAYS *"MY MOTHER"* gives me chills. Really, it does. The two words are anger edged in pain, and I am fully, sharply awake.

Eva is different in the dark, which is true of most people, but this is different. For one thing, she's holding my hand so tight I'm losing circulation. But she doesn't seem to notice it. She's watching the water like something might emerge from the tiny nighttime ripples and drag itself, gasping, over the sand.

Maybe I'm the one who's different in the dark.

"You know, it was so many years ago that it shouldn't matter, but...." Her voice is trembling now. When I first came out here, she sounded contemplative, like she was slowly turning over ideas for her book in her mind after a long day. I get that feeling. I've sat in parks near apartments and hostels all over the world, going through the day's mistakes and the next day's plans.

This is not that feeling.

Eva hesitates, her free hand coming up to brush at the corner of her eye. "I haven't thought about it in a long time. There's no need to—"

"Tell me. I swear to God, Eva, whatever it is, I can take it."

She laughs bitterly. "I'm the one who can't take it. I'm the one who's still thinking about it days and months and years later, like a stupid child who can't get over the fact that...."

I'm actually going to lose my hand. My fingers are in imminent danger. I raise both our hands to my lips and plant a kiss at the base of her thumb.

Eva makes a frustrated noise. "You can't do that. You can't just...override my brain like that."

"I'm sorry. I'll never do it again." I start to pull my hand away and she holds on tight.

"It's over and done," Eva says, mostly to herself, and then she sucks in a deep breath and lets it out. "My sister was always the perfect one. You know how that is."

"I don't have any siblings, but I've seen plenty of movies."

"She really was," Eva insists. "She was everything my parents wanted. She was so smart, and so dedicated, and so...*everything* that I could never compete. Not that I wanted to, unless it came to.... This isn't making any sense."

The sound of the night presses in around us, but every time Eva speaks again, all the noise settles. It's like the entire world is listening to her, and I'm only part of it. It's the opposite of how I felt in Afghanistan, when they'd send me out on patrol. It was always dark on the overnight shift, there at the edge of the FOB. Back then, I was the one trying to listen to the world, trying to hear who was sneaking under cover to plant the next seed of chaos. Sometimes it would be them. Sometimes it would be us. But it was always chaos.

"My mom was sitting next to one of her aunts, with my sister on the other side of her. At first, I wasn't following the conversation, because all of them were talking at once, and it was such a nice sound, all those voices by the fire." A little smile flickers across her face and disappears. "And I don't know why I caught what she said, but my aunt said something, and my mom said, '*Eva might never catch up with Emily. She's just too different. Off, sometimes.*' That's what she said."

Eva presses her lips together and lifts her chin.

What the hell am I supposed to say to that?

What the hell was her mom thinking? I'm not one of those judgmental dicks who's going to have an opinion on every word that comes out of a parent's mouth, but with her other daughter sitting there? Christ. I used to live across the street from two brothers named James and Carl, and it's a miracle that James, the younger one, made it out alive. It doesn't sound like that's what happened with Eva's parents. It doesn't sound nearly that extreme. But I guess you never know what goes on behind closed doors. Maybe this is just the tip of the iceberg.

She lets out a short, sharp breath and I think she might shake it off, stand up, go back inside, but instead, Eva claps her hand to her mouth to cover a ragged sob.

I'm out of the chair faster than I've ever done anything, including running for cover in Afghanistan.

I go to my knees in front of her.

She cries and cries, and there's nothing to do but be there for her, and it fills me with adrenaline and a new kind of strength.

"You've probably seen way worse." Eva's face is puffy in the moonlight, her green eyes colorless but bright. "Way worse things, just from traveling and the army." She shakes her head. "And here I am, blubbering about something my mother never intended for me to hear. It's so fucking stupid."

"It's not.

"It *is*. It's one of those things I should have left in the past a long time ago. I shouldn't be bothering people with dumb shit like this."

A laugh wends its way up and out of my mouth. "Do you ever bother anyone about anything? I mean, really. I'd bet all the money in my bank account that you never told Whitney why you left her party."

She scowls at me. "Whitney doesn't need to be burdened with—"

I cup her face with my hands. "The people who love you don't consider this kind of thing a burden."

"The people who love me...." Eva's eyes going wide. "Don't make promises you can't keep, Ben."

It's a warning, undeniably true; I shouldn't make promises I can't keep. I shouldn't pretend that the things I need to know won't take me away from her. But right here, right now, I'm seeing her. She's the rawest she's ever been, and I know without a shadow of a doubt that I will always want to explore her. Her mind. Her body. Her soul. No matter what takes me away, the beautiful mystery of her will always bring me back.

"What would be so terrible about making promises?"

Eva looks into my eyes, and I swear I can see her hope and anguish battling it out. "It always ends up being a burden. Sometimes one that's too heavy to carry."

"There's nothing too heavy for me to carry." I flex one arm to support my point. "I never gave up my army fitness."

Eva looks at me skeptically. "You don't know what you're getting into."

"Because you won't *let* me know what I'm getting into. It's not like I can torture it out of you."

"There are probably ways."

This is a serious conversation, and Eva's face is still streaked with tears. But there's a curl in her voice that reminds me of the bedroom and the pink in her cheeks at the fact of me looking at her in broad daylight. "If you still think torture is all about pain, then I've neglected you on this...retreat."

She sighs. "See? This is the problem. Every time I get close to this...past bullshit, you're there with your pretty face and your—" Her eyes flick down to the front of my pants, where there's an undeniable bulge. "—manly ways, and I end up thinking that more sex with you is going to solve everything."

"Eva." I've never been more serious about anything in my life. "There's only one way to know if more sex with me will solve all your problems." I lean in and taste the salt of her tears on one cheek then the other. She tilts her lips up and catches my lips with hers on the way back through.

"Only one?"

I pretend to consider it. "You're right, more than one.

You could be on your knees, on your back, bent over the bed...."

She puts a hand to my chest, right over my heart. "But what happens when it gets too dangerous?"

"Are you saying *you're* too dangerous for *me*?" The idea is laughable. I am the one who will hurt Eva, because I'm the one who's always being pulled to one side of the country or another, or worse, the opposite side of the globe. And not for my work—for myself. I have to know how things fit together. And you can't go to war without becoming aware of how they *all* fit together. All my projects—all my searching—will always lead me on to the next thing. That's the nature of the beast.

"You have no idea how dangerous I am." There's no more playfulness in her voice. "I'm serious, Ben. I—"

"I don't care." There's no more playfulness in mine, either. "I don't know how to be any clearer about it. When I look at you..." When I look at Eva, I'm convinced there's no greater mystery in the world. And I know that even if I figured all of it out—even if I knew every single thing there was to know about her—I'd still want to know more. It's a bright, pulsing need at the center of my core. "I want you," I say simply. "I want to be with you. I'd have driven you home a long time ago if this wasn't what I wanted."

"You can't possibly know that," she insists, her voice barely above a whisper. "You can't possibly feel that—"

"I felt it when I saw you at that party. I felt it when you slept in my bed. And I sure as *hell* felt it when that truck was coming at us. Are you saying that's not real?"

"I'm saying the consequences might be more than you're prepared for."

"And what are the consequences, Eva? I've had a broken heart before. I can survive it again."

Eva looks down into her lap then back up at me. "I don't want to break your heart. I want..."

"Tell me."

"I want to stay with you. For, like, as long as I live."

She might as well have shoved me over the cliff with her own two hands, because I'm falling hard. Harder than I've ever fallen before, for anything. No, not falling. I've fallen. If my knees weren't already on the ground, they'd be bruised from the impact.

Eva leans forward at the same time I do, and this time, there are no more tears on her cheeks to kiss away.

There are only her willing lips inviting me to taste her. So I do. God, I do, with the moonlight falling down in a silver sheet over us and the night wind stirring the leaves in the trees.

When Eva makes a little noise in the back of her throat that's somewhere between a moan and a sigh, I know it's time to go back inside.

I lift her in my arms for the hell of it and she laughs, the sound bouncing off the front of the cabin, her moment of joy multiplied. I feel her lips on my neck, her kiss light and hot, and it's so different from the way she tried to hold me at arm's length that my mind can't make the two things work together.

"You're like that Katy Perry song."

"Yes. I am a firework," Eva says haughtily.

"No. That old one." I reach out with one hand and open the storm door then kick the screen door open so we can step inside. "The hot and cold, yes and no thing."

"Deep cuts," Eva jokes. "I didn't take you for a fan."

I set her on her feet and kiss her again. Yeah. All of our clothes are coming off as soon as possible. I'm sure that's in another Katy Perry song somewhere. "Are you like this with your family too? Or do you save all this mental whiplash just for me?"

Eva's head is tilted up, and the moon is shining fully in through the front window, so I see the sad little smile that rises and falls on her face. "Oh, no. I don't have a family anymore."

19

BENNETT LOOKS WINDED, like all the air has been sucked right out of the cabin and there's no emergency oxygen mask. "Shit, Eva." He runs a hand through his hair, keeping the other one at my waist, and the pressure of it there, somehow both light and possessive at the same time, makes something inside of me twist and ache and heat. "Honestly, fuck. I'm sorry. I think."

This is the part I hate about letting people in on this life detail. I hate it so much that my chest goes numb and my fingertips go cold. This is a place I don't want to be in. Ever. "I didn't run away from home or anything. It was a car accident."

"Fuck."

"When I was nine."

Ben takes a deep breath and studies me. "Then you've heard all the bullshit people have to say. I won't add to it. "

Oh, what sweet, sweet relief. I take both of Ben's hands and raise his knuckles to my lips then kiss every single one of them. This—this swooning, lightheaded feeling, along with a genuine beat of *I'm so impressed*—is the closest I've ever felt to the kind of head-over-heels love you see in the movies. Not that the bar should be that low for Ben, or any man. But no one other than Whitney has said anything so frank in response to this revelation.

"Is this part of the terrible consequences of being with you?" He says it with a husky laugh in his voice.

"This is a thank you."

"For what?"

"For not saying '*they're in a better place now.*'"

Ben shakes his head, scowling in a way that says *I wouldn't ever say something so stupid.* "You know, after I got out of the army, people used to say that to me about my buddies who didn't make it back." He breathes out sharply through his nose. "It doesn't matter if they're in a better place, when it feels like you've got a stab wound through the chest. That shit was almost as bad as when my dad died."

Oh—*oh.*

I move in closer and trace one of his lips with my fingertip, hyperaware of every beat of my own heart, very much alive in large part thanks to this man. "When did he die?"

"What?" The corner of Ben's mouth curves upward. "You're not going to tell me how sorry you are?"

I tilt my face up toward his and kiss him with all the pain that's in my heart. It never goes away when someone you love dies. Never. It's always there, aching with every heartbeat, like a cut that won't heal. A stubborn cut. One you keep going to the doctor about, and they say *"as long as you're not bleeding to death, you'll live"* and shrug you out of the office. Some days it's easier to tolerate the mess. Sometimes it's like a fresh stab wound. There's nothing to do but keep living with it. Even so, I still have room to feel the hurt that echoes in Ben too.

I'm sorry, I tell him in my mind as I lick that bottom lip and draw it in between my teeth. *I'm sorry for what happened to you, but I'm not sorry to be here with you, even though I should be, because I'll only cause you more pain.*

The thought starts to burrow its way into the center of my brain, and I squeeze my eyes shut tighter. If I let it get too far, it's going to shut down all the progress I've made. Better to leave it lurking in the future, which, as we both know, may never get here at all.

I don't have another choice, because Ben is done with apologies. He's done with soft kisses and sorrowful little breaths. It's the middle of the dark and the cabin is soaked with pale moonlight, and the look in his eyes shifts from searching to needing. "Come back to bed," he growls.

"Take me there," I tell him.

He does.

———

"You're good at changing the subject."

Ben stirs, unhooking his arm from around my waist and rolling onto his back. It's darker in the bedroom than the living room, so—woe is me—I have to feel for his abs in the dark instead of seeing them with my own two eyes. I skim the hard muscles with my fingertips and explore down to where the sheet is in a tangled line at his hips.

"I can't help that sex like that sends me into the sweet embrace of sleep."

"I'm not talking about *that* subject."

He takes in a deep, even breath and lets it out slowly. "Name the subject. Any subject. I swear, I'll stay on track. You have my complete focus."

I slip my fingers beneath the sheet and graze the fine curls there. Ben groans, lifting his hips. "That's warfare."

"I'm helping you focus."

"You haven't asked me a question yet."

I leave my hand where it is and rest my head against his shoulder. "You never told me when your dad died."

He gathers me in, looping his fingers gently around my wrist to hold it in place. "That's really what you want to talk about? Right now?"

"It's dark."

Ben huffs a laugh. "You're right. In the daylight, I'm too busy spreading—"

I twist my wrist in his grip just for show. "You promised."

All I hear for a little while is the sound of Ben breathing. It's so level and rhythmic that it relaxes me against my will, carrying my mind neatly away from this golden opportunity and into—what did he call it?—the sweet embrace of sleep.

"Two years ago."

I'm so far gone that at first I don't know what he's talking about, but then it all clicks neatly into place. "Was it...sudden?"

"It felt sudden, but it wasn't." I thought it wasn't possible for our bodies to get any closer, but Ben proves me wrong. "I was...traveling a lot at the time, and he died right after I got back to the States."

"I mean, you have to know this raises a ton of questions."

"Does it?"

"Was your dad sick?"

Another little sigh. I know this pain intimately. So, so intimately. "Lung cancer."

"Shit." When I was in middle school, I had a friend named Autumn whose dad died after several years of fighting some kind of cancer. I assume it must have been testicular, because adults never wanted to say that in front of anyone from my age set. I'll never forget how bitter that tasted. Everyone told Autumn and her family the usual bullshit, only they got to say how glad they were for those extra few years with him. It only occurred to me later that every year we get with someone is an extra year. In middle school, I only wished I could be Autumn. At least, I thought, I'd still have a mom left. But now, lying here with Ben, I see it more clearly. His mother left without a backward glance, and she probably didn't have cancer.

"Yeah. He never smoked, which was—" Ben laughs. "It was one of his pet peeves, people smoking. He did a stint in the army too, so you'd think...."

"Did you smoke in the Army?"

"Hell no. I didn't want to get lung cancer." He breathes in and out, and it's so steady and healthy I can't even picture it.

"Yeah. Maybe I should avoid cars."

Ben is silent for a moment. "Is this because of that semi truck? Because if you ask me, it's trucks you should be wary of."

This, of all moments, is the moment that I should tell him what happened. I should lie here in the dark and give him all the details. Not that I was there for any of the details; I only heard about them afterward, second-hand, in the way that you tell a nine-year-old about the greatest tragedy of her life.

But I don't want to.

And it's not because of the intense urge that follows me everywhere I go, to keep the heartache hidden. It's because *I'm* here for *Ben*. If I can just keep my mouth shut about it—about what *really* happened—he'll see me for a person who's here for him.

Who loves him.

He'll never know what a risk he's taking, wanting to be with me like this. And God, I want him too. I want to lie here in the dark listening to the beat of his heart and the breath in his lungs until daylight, and then on into forever. Even if it means that he will eventually see all the ugliest parts of me.

But then, what hasn't a man like Bennett Powell seen? Can I really be uglier than war? Can I be needier than the army?

I follow those thoughts down a darkly wooded path until it's too hard to look at them, and then my mind drifts over to things like sandy beaches and lawn chairs and solid wood walls that keep out all the worst parts of the world. It drifts into that illusory knowledge that everything is fine, that everything will always be fine. In this lovely dream, the prospect of losing everyone who matters to me is somewhere in the far future. It's not the weight that anchors my past.

The rush of the waves on the sandy beach takes over. The sound is half real, amplified by the dream, so I miss what Ben says the first time.

I curl against him, tighter, tighter. "What?"

"I wasn't really there."

I hastily retrace the steps of our conversation. "For your dad, you mean?"

"Yeah." There's a catch in his breath that might as well be a gunshot. "I was in the Middle East. Afghanistan mostly."

"Deployed?"

"No."

"You went *back*?"

He gives a little sigh. "I spent eighteen months chasing answers about what happened that day in the Humvee. And during that eighteen months, my dad dealt with his cancer by himself."

My stomach twists.

"I asked him if I should come back every time we talked, and he always told me not to. I shouldn't have listened."

"Was work really that important?"

Another pause.

"I called it work. But really it was my own personal project, I guess you'd call it."

"You spent a year and a half overseas for that?"

Ben doesn't sound defensive at all when he answers me. "I'd planned on two. Things fell into place early. I had a contact in Kabul, a friend of a friend. He had more information than I thought. That's when I found the pieces."

"The pieces of what?"

"The pieces of the IED."

The way this knowledge sinks in is like an enormous boulder plummeting toward the surface of deep water, leaving behind the light as it falls.

That's how far he'll go.

I didn't understand until this moment that Bennett Powell is not only a man who sees. He *seeks*.

And there's very little that will stop him once he's decided on a goal.

The sheet pulled up around me is suddenly trapping ten times the heat, and it's too close. What would Bennett do if he found out about my family? What if he got to the bottom of that and discovered that it was really me all along who was at the heart of the tragedy?

This can't last, a voice in the back of my mind whispers. *It can't, because every path leads to the same place.*

The forks in the road are only an illusion. The destination will always be that Bennett will look elsewhere for whatever he needs in this life.

I pull away from him with an exaggerated yawn and stretch my arms above my head.

"But I did find them," he says, almost to himself.

One breath in, one breath out.

That's how I pretend to be asleep.

20

I CAN'T TELL if this is the longest week of my life, the best week, or both.

It all seems dreamlike. A scene out of an action movie. Did that truck really almost hit us? Those first few moments of waking, I can hardly believe any of it happened. The thunderstorm. The semi. My brain accepts it; of course it does. I saw enough during my deployments to know that terrible things happen in the world, and sometimes we witness them.

There are terrible things, yes.

And then there's Eva, who is something else entirely.

We've had as much sex as we've had work. By rights, she should be dead to the world until noon, but she's up early this morning. The bed is empty when I open my eyes, and it gives me the strangest plummeting feeling, though there's nothing to be worried about.

The first thing I do is look out the window.

There she is. My stomach rights itself.

Down by the lake, in one of the lawn chairs, her hair in an enormous bun on the top of her head. I didn't feel her leave this morning. The conversation we had last night is hazy, but something about it itches at the back of my mind. Did I say something that upset her? I don't see how I could have. It was nothing but the truth. Still, the set of her shoulders makes me think I did. But it could just be her focus on the story.

She has this way of tilting her head an inch to one side then the other, and I can tell by the way she's doing it now that she's deep in her writing.

I could watch her like this all day.

But that would be fucking creepy.

So I open up my email.

There's another little piece of a project from work, and just by the instructions, I know it won't take me more than an hour. A bunch of emails from businesses reminding me to seize the weekend. A reminder about tomorrow's meet-up for trivia.

And a response.

From that genealogy site.

I'd almost forgotten I'd sent a message to the owner of the page, but I'll be damned. I did, and they wrote back.

The name on the email is Cindy Siverling. She was one of the daughters listed on the page. My dad's sister. An aunt I never knew about. We were on our own after my mother left. His parents both died before I hit high school.

My pulse races.

This is a new lead that could take me all the way back to Michigan.

It hits me full force when I hover the mouse of the email—the urge to *move*.

In this moment, I want nothing more than to throw all my shit in a bag, jump in the rental car, and leave it behind at the nearest airport. I'd rather sit on a plane with three layovers if it means being in flight at all.

But things are more delicate now.

I can't just leave her out there in the sun. It was a risk for her, admitting that she needs me here, and I can't betray it.

Open the email; that's the first thing. I can't make any decisions about anything until I've opened the damn thing and read it.

Click.

Wait for it to load.

I keep my expectations absolutely neutral. That's something I learned in the army. No high hopes. No dread, either.

Dear Bennett,

I'm sorry to be the one to give you this news, but my father, Robert, died last month. It was very peaceful and he was surrounded by family. So you won't be able to ask him any questions.

I'm also sorry to be the one to tell you that my amateur genealogy attempts weren't...entirely correct.

"Am I interrupting?"

I have nothing to hide—nothing at all—and yet my first instinct is to reach up and close the laptop. Quickly. Eva stands in the doorway to the bedroom, face pink from the sun. Her smile isn't nearly big enough to conceal the way her eyebrows pull together, creating a worried line across her forehead.

"You're interrupting the very scintillating checking of emails. Frankly, I'm glad you came." I push the laptop onto the bed and throw my legs over the side. "I'm assuming you're here to deal," I say faux-seriously. "What do you already have to bargain with for breakfast?"

"Is it another...personal project?"

It comes back to me in bits and pieces, what I told her last night.

And still, those bits and pieces don't add up to this kind of concern.

It doesn't matter. She's asked me directly, and I've promised to tell the truth.

"Yes. Something else I'm working on."

Eva nods, and I can tell she's weighing her words carefully.

"Ask it, Eva. Whatever it is, you can ask it."

Her eyes are huge and luminous and wary. "Is it about me? Your project. Does it have to do with me?" She swallows so hard I can hear it. "Because if it has to do with me, you shouldn't do that. You should just stop. It's not a good idea to go down that path, and what you find—"

"Eva."

"—you're not going to like it, okay? And... fuck. This is probably one of the best weeks of my life, being here with you. I can't remember the last time I dropped everything and skipped town. Even if I'd *had* the balls to skip town, which I have not, it would have felt like I was running away from something. But with you, it feels like I'm running toward something, so if you're—"

It's two steps to get to her, and the instant I fold her in my arms, she goes quiet, her body relaxing. There's not a tense muscle in her when she presses her cheek into my chest.

For a minute.

Then her shoulders go back up.

"Are you hugging me so I'll shut up?"

"I'm hugging you, because I want to be close to you." It's true. But there are other truths too. "And I'm hugging you, because I might be able to kiss your mouth into silence, but not your brain. As long as you're thinking it, I want to hear about it."

"In, like, a *personal project* kind of way?"

I take a half step back and look into her eyes. "Why are you so hung up on that?"

"I don't know." Eva shrugs, but the worry is still painted onto her face. "Isn't it weird? I mean, isn't it a weird thing to do? To spend eighteen months on a single research project?" She doesn't add *when your father is dying*. She doesn't have to. "Is this... is this all you really want to be doing?"

"I didn't bring you here so I could spend all my time working on a secret project, if that's what you're trying to ask."

"No. That's not it."

"Then what?" I take her hands in mine. They're small, her bones fine, but her grip is solid. "And what do you mean, I won't like what I find? I want to know everything about you, yes. I'll admit that. But isn't that par for the course when you're falling for someone?"

Eva shakes her head briskly. "When you're falling for someone—"

Her mouth falls open.

"Did you—" She blinks like she's coming awake, like she's surfacing from deep water. "Did you say that out loud, or did I hallucinate it?"

It makes me laugh. God help me, it makes me laugh. "Is it so hard to believe?"

"We've known each other for seven days."

"It only took one night to know I never wanted you to leave my bed."

Eva giggles, a little burst of laughter that's totally uncharacteristic of her. "But that's impossible. That's…. You have no idea what you're getting into."

"Don't I?"

I let the question hang in the air between us for several heartbeats. Eva doesn't answer.

"I think I've got a pretty good grip on what I'm getting into. For one thing, you can't jump to save your life even if a semi truck is coming at you."

"That's not *fair*. I have…. It was a *truck,* and I—"

"For another, you're about as good at sharing your feeling as you are at jumping out of the way of speeding trucks."

Eva grimaces at me. "It's not something people should get into, because...."

"Because *why*? Jesus. Do they use your feelings to determine the nuclear launch codes? Are they some state secret? Is that why you're worried I might have taken you on as a side gig for my own sick pleasure?"

"It's not that sick of a pleasure." It's almost too soft to hear.

"It's not sick at all. It's fucking delicious. Being with you is almost too sweet to bear."

She cocks her head to the side. "I don't believe you. I can be...a difficult person. Not sweet at all."

"I've never met a writer who was easy to deal with when they were under deadline pressure. Most of you are like bottled lightning when you're under pressure."

"Yeah, well, what if I'm always under deadline pressure? Or what if this—" Eva motions between the two of us. "—thing we have only lasts as long as I have a problem I need help solving? Ugh. That makes me sound like a damsel in distress, and I am *not* in distress. I'm only—"

"You seem a little distressed right now."

"That's because you're in here chipping away at some secret file about yours truly."

"It's not about you. All right? It's about me. Does that make you feel better?"

She raises one eyebrow.

"Bennett. Are you obsessed with yourself?"

"Jesus Christ, no. Though now that you put it that way...."

"*You* are your own personal research project?" She looks mildly horrified.

"Oh my God, it's not that. There are things in my life that I want to know more about, and I can't go directly to the source, because the source is dead."

"What things?"

"How much have you written already this morning? I'll tell you for—"

"You'll tell me for nothing, Bennett Powell, and you'll like it."

I take a step back, completely unable to stop the wide grin from spreading across my face.

There is more to Eva Lipton than I could ever know. In seven days, she's been transformed from a pale, shaking shell of a woman to the fierce queen standing in front of me. These little moments of bravery give me a sudden rush of blood to below my waist.

Her scowl fades the more I smile until she's less fierce queen and more tentative queen, but still. *Still.*

"I demand to know." She puts both hands on her hips. Eva's really reaching for it this time, digging her heels in, and I get another rush that's not so different from vertigo.

"Okay. I'm…. That was amazing. That's one of my all-time favorite things you've ever said; let me just start with that."

She snaps her fingers between us. "No. I'm not letting this get sidetracked. The project."

"The project is about my father."

"That's it? Like, his family history? Are you putting together a family tree for your eventual…offspring?"

A delicate blush colors Eva's cheeks at the word. I

resist the powerful urge to ask her about *her* eventual offspring and shove away the mental image of a pregnant Eva, writing outside in the sun with a laptop propped on her belly.

"Like why he wanted me to join the army so badly, even though he left after his first contract was up. Spent the rest of his life working as a floor manager at a local company that produced windows. I want to know what made him that way."

"You never asked?"

Eva waits.

"You never asked."

"I never asked."

"So you're asking now."

"Yeah."

She shakes her head. "But Bennett...who's left to ask?"

21

Oʜ, thank God. Thank God, thank God.

The relief is so powerful I could sink to my knees with it. I've never done drugs, so I wouldn't know anything about mainlining...well, anything, but I assume it would be at least as good as this. It's like all my blood has been taken out and replaced with sweet wine.

Bennett's eyes light up when I ask the question, but he quickly tamps it down. "I don't need to bother you with this. If you're in the middle of a good scene, I'm not going to derail you with—"

"My scene is...fine." I'm so glad that he's not digging into my stupidly tragic past that I can hardly remember where I am in the book. I've been typing the same sentence for about ten minutes, trying to convince myself that Bennett would never... he would *never*... he didn't bring me here to do that. He would never.

I'm halfway through the story. Things are getting real. That's all I know.

In this moment, my relief is translated to an intense interest in also knowing exactly what Ben's been working on, if not, you know, me. I clear my throat and try not to dwell on the fact that *falling for me* might mean the way I feel about him is also okay. Allowable. Acceptable. Even though I know with all my heart that it is not. It will only lead to heartbreak. "Are there other family members you can...interview, I guess?"

He's falling for me wars with *he's not researching you* in my mind in an endless loop.

"Okay, so..." Ben rushes back to the bed and picks up his laptop. He opens the screen, and right there on the desktop is his email. He clicks over to another tab in his browser. "I'd already gone through all of his available medical records and everything in the house, since I had to pack it up for renters. And there is *nothing* there about why he might have been so attached to the army. But while we were here, I found this."

Ben brandishes the laptop at me, but we're faced with the inevitable hardship of trying to read off a screen that someone else is holding, so I take the computer out of his hands and sit down on the bed. My heart beats too fast for me to focus, so I will it to slow down. Be cool. Pretend you're doing your own research for a book.

But this is just one of the genealogy websites with a strip of ads on one side and a 1990s text-based jumble of words in the center.

"I...don't know what I'm looking at. Is this a random family tree?"

"It's my dad's family tree. His original family."

"Original?"

"He was adopted." Ben's eyes are bright and focused on the screen as if he might find another clue even while we're sitting here. "I found out this week. He was *adopted*."

"You found that out from this page?"

"No. I found that out from the private investigator I hired."

"Ben, what the fuck?" I close the lid of the laptop. "You hired a private investigator to find out why your dad wanted you to join the army? There's no way she can find an answer to some whim that was in his head."

"That's not why I hired her. Not exactly."

"Not exactly?"

He moves my hand gently off the lid of the laptop and opens the screen again. Ben deftly swipes at the mouse pad and clicks a few more times, opening a folder on the desktop. Inside the folder is an image file. He opens that too.

My heart hammers in my chest as the file opens to a white screen then slowly loads. I'm gripped with a sudden fear that I might be about to witness some weird crime scene photo, and I'm...not in the mood for an actual crime scene to be in front of my eyes at this moment.

"Sorry. This computer is a piece of shit sometimes."

"Yeah, mine too."

"It is not. You have last year's MacBook Pro model. That's a good machine."

"Shh."

"Did you just shush me?" Ben nudges me with his elbow as the picture comes fully into view.

It's an older photo that looks like it was printed out and scanned in, the color slightly faded. And the photo is of a little boy in a red sweater and brown corduroy pants. He can't be more than three or four, five at the most. It takes no time at all to recognize Ben's eyes.

"Is this you?"

"That's my dad."

We both look at the screen. Something must be crucial about this image, judging from the charged energy in the air, but I don't know what it is. And maybe Ben's still searching for clues in it.

The scene looks pretty set for Christmas Day. The little boy in the photo stands next to a toboggan the exact color of his sweater, beaming. He still has his baby teeth, and he honestly looks so happy he could pass out. Behind him, the lights hung on a Christmas tree have been sharpened to little points of dull color by the flash. In the corner behind him there's a slash of torn wrapping paper.

He looks so happy.

But I'm missing something—I have to be.

"You hired a private investigator because of this photo?"

"Yeah."

"I don't get it. Your parents must have lots of pictures, even though this was back in the day."

"This is the *only* photo they had of him."

I turn to look at Ben, who is still looking at the photo on the screen. "Were they anti-camera people?"

"No. What I mean is, this is the only photo they have of him before the age of fourteen."

"That's specific."

"That's when he was adopted."

I look back at the picture. The pieces are slow to fit into place. I'm too bogged down with story details and weird fears about Bennett Powell becoming a private investigator I never want to cross paths with. "So this was taken by his birth family?"

"Yes."

"Okay, but how can you know that?"

Now he's watching me. "When my father's parents died—and believe me when I say he *never* mentioned having a family other than his parents—we moved everything out of the house. We sold most of the furniture or donated it. He didn't keep any clothes. All he kept were some of the dishes and all the documents they kept in their filing cabinet, plus boxes of photos and other paperwork. On the weekends, he would go through and sort out which things could be thrown away and which needed to be kept."

"So he could have thrown away some of them by accident."

Ben shakes his head. "He was careful. He went through them paper by paper. He didn't make any mistakes with this."

"But how did *you* make the leap from this photo to private investigator?"

"Because I had to do the same thing when my father died, only I didn't leave the project for the weekends. I took my work with me and went through everything during the evenings."

"You literally went through every piece of paper in your dad's house?"

"I didn't have a choice." For the first time I can remember, Ben looks haunted. "There were...life insurance matters to be sorted out. Accounts to cancel and transfer. I still don't know what to do with the money he left me. He must have saved it for years.

"But that's not what I was there for—money. I was trying to understand why he was fine with being so alone. And instead, I found this." Ben leans back onto his elbows on the bed. "It stuck out to me. I had gone over pictures that day, and that night. I couldn't sleep. Something was weird about them, you know?"

Goose bumps rise up and down my arms. "This sounds like something I'd write into a book."

"I know. I almost expected to see something creepy as fuck when I got up and went through them again."

"In the middle of the night?"

"In the middle of the night."

"You're brave."

"Army Strong," he jokes. "Anyway, it was somewhere around dawn when I finally figured out what I was seeing. Something wasn't right. Why would his parents only have pictures of him from age fourteen on? No teenager wants a camera anywhere near them, so it would be strange as hell to *start* taking pictures then."

I think of all the photos my aunt and uncle took of me

growing up. They were never the kind to want kids, and I never thought we were particularly close, but for my high school graduation, my uncle stayed up late four nights in a row and made giant collages of all my school pictures. They must have had hundreds, but from all ages. He included my parents and my sister whenever he could.

I don't know if I loved him for that or hated him.

"Yeah. That is odd."

"And before you ask, there was never a house fire, or a stray safety deposit box—nothing. I asked my great aunt. She let me go through her photos too. There was nothing."

"What did she say? About the adoption?"

"Nothing."

"She said *nothing*? I don't believe that. Old ladies always have opinions."

Ben grins. "She wasn't that old when we had that conversation. But she was pretty tight-lipped about what her sister had done. Wouldn't give an inch."

"But why...." I push the laptop back toward him. "No. You're not getting me sucked into this."

"I tried to keep you *out* of this. Remember?"

"Well, *now* I won't be able to stop thinking about it. Is that all there was? No. There was something else. An email?"

He turns the screen back toward me and clicks over to his browser again. "This is the genealogy information that I got based on what the private investigator had uncovered. This was his birth family. For some reason, he was adopted out of the foster system at the age of fourteen, but they went on to have two other children. Does that make sense to you?"

"I don't know what makes sense." The names and dates on the screen are utterly meaningless. "If this were a thriller, I'd be *very* interested in them. But I don't know what they could possibly tell you."

"That's the email I just got. I wrote to one of them."

"You wrote to one of these random people and asked them why your father wanted you to join the army, even though he only stayed in for one contract?"

Ben looks at me like I've just dropped in from another planet. "Of course not. I only asked if the father would be willing to talk to me. But he's dead." He says this matter-of-factly. "One of my dad's sisters is not. She set up the page. She's the one who wrote me the email."

"What did it say?"

"I've only read about half. The first half wasn't good news, but the second half still has promise."

It makes no sense at all, absolutely none, but I'm gripped by the fear that whatever is in that email will take him away from me, and I can't stand it. I feel like that semi truck is coming at me again. It's pushing the wind so forcefully it blows my hair away from my face, only this time I'm the one who has to do something—anything—to stop it.

"Read it later." I put my palms on Ben's carved chest and push him backward toward the bed, my heart pounding. He's intoxicating like this, with that half-sleepy grin on his face, his blond hair tousled, still warm from being between the sheets. "We have other plans."

22

BENNETT

SEX LEADS TO A LATE, lingering breakfast, which leads to more sex, which leads to a lunch that Eva eats draped in a white sheet from the bed. Her hair is a wreck. I love it that way. I *made* it that way.

She watched me cook it in my boxers, her eyes dutifully trained on my face whenever I turned around. I'm sure she was looking elsewhere when I was facing the stove. God knows the sheet is enough to drive me crazy. It has a mind of its own, that sheet, slipping over her skin and dipping into places I want to touch.

When I finally sit down, I've been rigid for what seems like hours. There should be some kind of medal given out for being able to cook a decent meal.

And it *is* decent. It's more than decent, for a stir-fry. I fucking *nailed* the chicken. I know it the moment Eva takes her first bite. She can't stand chicken that's not perfect. Oh, she'll try to hide it, but seven days of staring at her face has given me enough insight to know there are certain things she can't help. Like the way she grimaces ever so slightly if she doesn't like the food.

As much as I want her, I am also after-sex hungry. Ravenous. Maybe that's why the chicken tastes so good.

"It's good," she says.

"Nay," I tell her. "It's perfect."

We work our way through our plates, and I focus as much attention as possible on the shadows of the leaves on the counter and not the fall of the sheet over Eva's body.

She spears a section of red pepper with her fork and slips it between her lips. I've never seen anyone chew anything more thoughtfully than she is right now, her gaze leveled at me across the countertop.

"Like what you see?"

"Yeah." Her fork hits the countertop with a muted

clink. Eva's voice is cool, like she's used to looking at me this way, but I see the way the blush curls across her cheeks. She couldn't hide it from me if she wanted to.

I hope she never wants to.

"I think we should leave," Eva announces.

"What?"

The day is stretching into the kind of golden afternoon that we could spend entirely in bed. I was also considering a swim. I wouldn't mind a race out to the buoy and then, while we kicked in place, far from the shore and far from any lurking boats, I could slip the tie of her bikini top loose and watch that water lap over the curves of her breasts.

And now she wants to leave?

Eva gets up from the counter, sweeping the sheet regally around her body. "You got to plan our whole...arrival. I want to plan our departure."

"Are you done with your book?"

She's gone into the second bedroom. "Halfway done. That's more progress than I've made in months. I'm not worried about finishing it in the city."

I get up and follow her, leaning against the doorframe to the second bedroom. Eva, the sheet still draped around her shoulders, delicately puts clothes into her bag. Tidiness has not been a priority in the second bedroom, but she works fast, like we're up against a deadline.

"You're serious."

"I'm serious." Eva looks up at me with a playful smile. "We should get back to the city."

"For what?"

"For the meet-up tomorrow."

"The meet-up?"

"With your group." She steals a glance at me over her open suitcase. "I want to go with you."

"You *do*?" The Eva I met a week ago was doing her level best to get the hell out of a social gathering. It doesn't make sense that she's so desperate to go back. I do have a certain...prowess, but that's not enough to do *this*.

"I do. I really do." Eva stands up tall and adjusts the sheet around her shoulders. The front falls open in places and I can see through to her skin. Just the hint of it is enough to make me want to take her directly back to bed. "Clearly, shutting myself away from everyone wasn't helping the writing process. And, you know, we're going to have to go back eventually." She raises her eyebrows. "Unless you are a secret, rich prince who prefers to slum it in commoners' summer cabins. Or! Maybe you secretly own this place. You should tell me now, if you do, because I would totally come back. Later."

She picks up the pace, putting more things into the suitcase.

"What's the rush?"

"You don't want to go to the meet-up? It's a trivia night. It sounds fun."

"The fact that *you* want to go there is a little bit..."

"Surprising? Well, surprise. I am in fact a multifaceted woman with varied interests, not just a panic monster who likes to dance in the rain."

"I like the panic monster who wants to dance in the rain." Eva crooks an eyebrow at me. "With a little less panic monster, sure. But only because I hate seeing you all drawn and pinched like that. And I'm anti-getting-struck-by-lightning."

"Admit it. The post-rain sex was the hottest thing ever in your life."

"Oh, God, Eva, I can't rank all of our sexual encounters here. That would destroy my brain. But...if you want to, I guess we can sit down with some paper, and—"

"No." She stands up tall. "We need to get going. We have to get back to the city."

"You know it's Friday, right? The trivia night isn't until tomorrow."

Eva nods solemnly. "We'll need a day to...decompress. We can't show up like we just rolled out of bed. And you know as well as I do that if we stay until tomorrow, we'll stay until the last possible moment, roll out of bed, and show up smelling like—"

"Sunscreen and lake water?"

"Like we've spent a week doing sex bargaining."

I go across and stop her before she can put anything else into the suitcase. "Has there not been enough sex bargaining? Because I'll make you a deal right now if you stop packing."

Eva bites her lip, her eyes flickering down to the front of my boxers. "You're only delaying the inevitable."

"Let me." I take her face in my hands and kiss her. Whatever this is—whatever fear or reservation or hesitation—I want to drown it in love. "Give me two more hours. You won't regret it."

Her head is tipped back, the sheet slipping from her shoulders. It takes me exactly one roll of her nipple between my fingertips to make her putty in my hands.

"When you say it like *that*, it sounds less like a deal and more like an order."

"Mmm. I think you like it when I give orders." I bend my head and bite along her collarbone, leaving the ghosts of teeth marks on her skin.

"I'm very independent," Eva insists, but she wraps her arms around my neck nonetheless. "Nobody can give me orders. Not even you."

"On the bed. Hands and knees."

Eva's eyes flash. I keep my expression deadly serious.

"*Now*."

She hesitates.

"If you can't follow orders, I'll have to help you." I take her wrists in my hands, turn her around, and lift her onto the bed. Eva sinks down immediately, her back arched, and I don't have to touch her to know she's already wet. I can see her glistening.

"Two hours," she whispers.

"I'll be the judge of that."

WE KEEP it to a tight five hours, including the time it takes to put the guest bedroom back into reasonable order *and* a shower that goes twenty minutes past Eva's five-minute deadline. The sun is setting by the time I do one last sweep of the cabin and find one of Eva's bra's peeking out from underneath the bed. I hang it over my shoulder while I put the key back in the lockbox and punch the code to lock it.

She's already waiting in the car, computer in her lap.

I open the driver side door and toss the bra in at her. It lands squarely in the middle of the keyboard.

"Oh my *God*. I'm trying to meet *your* deadline, and you're tossing lingerie at me?"

"It's yours. I found it under the bed."

Eva throws it back in my face, laughing. "Our bags are on the backseat. Put it in there, for God's sake."

I do. "What are you at now?"

"Twenty chapters down. I think I can wrap this up in another ten."

"With two weeks left to spare?"

Eva's hands pause on the keyboard and she purses her lips. "About that..."

I stop in the middle of checking the mirrors and tugging on the handle to make sure the door is securely closed. "Is the deadline farther out than you led me to believe? Because if you need false deadlines, I can set them up with the best of them."

"It's closer."

"Ah."

"I'm sorry I didn't tell you."

I put the car in reverse and maneuver us away from the front of the cottage. On little roads like this, people speed by without a second look, so there's no way I'm going out ass first. Especially not with Eva in the car. "None of my business." I try to flash her a reassuring grin, but she's staring out the window. I try to mean it, but something in my chest aches at the thought of Eva's life not being my business.

"You brought me here. It should have been your business." Her hands spring to life on the keyboard again. She types so fast that the sound of it makes me feel vaguely off-balance.

At least she's writing.

I don't say anything.

We pull out onto the dirt road that leads to the main road. The speed of her typing increases, reaches critical mass, and then Eva abruptly shuts the laptop. The *clap* of it hasn't fully processed in my brain before she shoves it into a bag in the back and settles in, still not looking at me.

I have to keep my eyes on the road. I take a right onto the main highway and accelerate up to the speed limit. Is it shame coming off her in waves? Regret that we're leaving? Sadness? I have my own little pit at the base of my gut from leaving the cabin. The cabin exists in its own little world. Being back in the city puts us right back where we started.

The sound of the wheels on the road gets louder the longer we sit in silence.

"Do you think you'll write on the way back?"

Eva turns and looks at me, and I get a flash of the downturned corners of her lips. "I would, but I'll get carsick."

"Being carsick is bullshit."

"Yeah," she says. "It is."

"There is a silver lining though."

"What's that?"

I steal another glance at her. She's framed by the window, surrounded by the summer green of the trees whipping by. I feel like all the time we've spent together is getting sucked back into the cosmic bottle it must have spilled out of, and when it's all back in, the lid will be shut tight, never to be opened again.

But that's out there, waiting for some other version of me. The version of me who's not driving the car.

I reach for her hand.

Eva takes mine with a little sigh under her breath that fills me with my own strange contentment. I'm not

used to being content. I'm used to being uncomfortable. To always reaching for the next thing. To always
having it being slightly out of my grasp.

Not today.

Today, everything I need is right here next to me.

It's in the palm of my hand.

23

EVA

I REGRET LEAVING the cabin the moment Ben closes my apartment door behind me.

Really, I regretted it the whole drive home. I regretted it from the moment I closed my laptop and put it away, and I regretted it every second he held my hand like we're together now, even though that will mean telling him the truth.

And once I tell him the truth, there's no coming back from it. He'll *know*.

I meant to tell him when he came in, carrying my bags. And then I meant to tell him when he wrapped me in his arms and kissed me goodbye. I even meant to tell him as he stood in the doorway, looking back, watching me with those dark eyes of his. I ached to tell him. But that cold, wretched fear already had its grip around my neck.

"I think I can finish the book tonight." I gave him the most confident smile I could manage.

Worry etched itself across his face. "If you're going to be up all night, I can stay. You'll need someone to bargain with when the going gets tough."

I was on the verge of saying *"yes, please stay. Stay forever."* But...

I don't.

Because I can't slip into this routine in New York City that we had at the cabin. I can't let it become commonplace. I can't let it feel as comfortable as my own sheets. If I do, I might not be able to let him go.

"I'm all right," I lied. "I just need one night to get everything set up for the big finale. And I'll see you at the trivia night tomorrow."

He leaned down and kissed me, the feel of his lips on mine like a sparkling firework running through my veins, and my heart grasped onto the feeling. *Stay,* it said. *Stay.*

But my mouth said, "Get going. You need a day to relax without me."

So now I'm here, in an apartment that feels too empty and strange. Everything is exactly where I left it. There's the pair of flip-flops I meant to pack and forgot next to the couch. The clean dishes are still in the drying rack. I was so meticulous about everything but writing my book.

And when Ben showed up with a way to run, I didn't hesitate.

No more.

I drag the bags back into my bedroom and dump them onto the bed. My laptop is right on top, where I left it during the drive, and I pick it up like a shield and carry it back over to my desk.

I sit down...

...open it up...

...and write.

It's a kind of fugue state, honestly. That's what it's like to get so deep into a story that you don't mind the pain in your wrists or the vague ache in your skull from not eating. The last time I had any tea was hours ago, and no plate has appeared by my elbow. That's the thing that brings me out of it—no plate. No food I can shovel ungraciously into my mouth while I peck out an outline between bites.

It's dark outside. I have enough of the book to send to Kayla on Monday. If I keep my ass in the chair most of tomorrow, it should be very nearly done.

It's been dark since we got back, but now it's *really* dark—the kind of dark that highlights exactly how much light pollution New Yorkers live under every day. The street outside has gone quiet, except for two men who are calling back and forth to each other from opposite corners, but the quiet doesn't seem right anymore.

It's all concrete and traffic, and my brain keeps straining to hear the wash of the lake on the beach.

I stand up and stretch my arms over my head, my shoulders aching. They never ached like this when I was working at the cabin.

Because of Ben.

Obviously.

It's so *obvious,* now that he's not here. All those deals we made were short-term. He never gave me enough time to sink into my own skeleton and let my muscles cramp and protest. A thousand words for a kiss. Another thousand for him to kneel between my legs and devour me. Two thousand, and he'd do it out in the yard, just because it feels electric when people might see. Three thousand and he'd pin me against the wall in the cabin, my shorts hanging off one ankle.

The truth is that I don't want to go to bed without him. Could anyone blame me? That warm, solid body next to mine was as much an anchor as it was a match to the tinder of my imagination.

"You did the right thing," I tell my reflection in the mirror, though I don't really believe it. What I do believe is that we were getting close to the event horizon of our relationship—the point at which all the light can no longer escape the gravity of our differences. He'd tried to give me all of him, and it sent me running back to the city.

You couldn't bear it. Not twice, that little voice in my mind whispers. *You need him, and you couldn't bear it if you killed him.*

Not like I killed the rest of them.

24

Two THINGS HAPPEN in the early morning.

I get a text from Eva, and I get an email from Cindy Siverling.

I read her first email when I got back to my apartment, feeling like I'd lost all the purpose in my life. It only occurred to me when I opened my laptop that Eva had planned this. She hadn't wanted to see what the email said in the first place, and she'd done her level best to delay it as long as possible.

Or maybe she really had needed to come back home.

Cindy's first email had ended in an offer to talk on the phone.

Then, this morning, another message:

**It might be best if we meet face-to-face. I'm
not sure I want to deliver these kinds of
details to you over the phone. If you're ever
in Michigan, please stop by and we can talk.**

She left her address and phone number too.

When I was at the cabin with Eva, flying back to
Michigan would have been a nonstarter. Why would I
ever get in a metal tube to be hurtled across the Great
Lakes and put all that distance between us? At the
cabin, she was the sun, and I was in orbit around her.

Twelve hours alone, and I'm already being pulled into
a new solar system.

There's no direct flight before 10:00 p.m., and as much
as my blood is humming to move, move, move, I don't
want to spend all day in the airport—Milwaukee,
specifically. And because she's not here, and because
I'm honestly not sure that she'll ever be here again, I
book that ten o'clock flight. I feel a little pang when I
realize this will mean cutting the trivia night short.

No. I won't even be able to go at all.

It's too far from the airport, and when you factor in
security....

This is going to mean disappointing Eva.

But the call is too strong.

And she is too far.

I write back to Cindy.

I have some things to take care of in the city, but I'll be in Michigan tonight. Please let me know when you have some time.

Done.

It's only then that I remember the text.

Eva: I missed you last night.

Ben: I missed you, too. How did writing go?

Eva: My shoulders are killing me.

Ben: You should find someone to barter massages with you.

Eva: I think I did find him, but for some reason I let him go back to his own place last night ???

My heart thrums in my throat. Her name on the screen might as well be a video of her at the lake, her hair shining in the sun, those red curls flying in the breeze. Eva, laughing in that too-small bikini.

What the hell am I thinking?

How can I disappoint her?

The answer, of course, is that I need to do both things. I need to meet with Cindy, and I need to see Eva. If I can make them both work, it'll be a sign.

Ben: Keep going. Finish that book.

Eva: How many words will it take to see you at the trivia night?

Ben: As many as you can.

Eva: I'll bring proof with me.

Ben: Good girl.

Eva: That's not fair.

Ben: All's fair in love and books.

And secrets, I think to myself.

There's a long pause. She must be writing, so I get up and strip. I can shower and get some errands done then pack for the airport.

Eva: Ben?

The phone vibrates just as I'm stepping into the shower. I get back out to look.

Ben: These don't count as words, by the way.

Eva: There's something we should talk about tonight.

Ben: I'm always up for a good talk. Write enough words, and I'll be an open book.

She doesn't say anything after that.

IT TURNS out that even when you work from home, skipping town for a solid week will leave you with a pile of things to do when you get back.

First: explain to all my buddies from the Warriors where I've been. Ash wants to know if I skipped town for another eighteen months to look for more shrapnel in the desert. Gunnar Langdon, another guy who always shows up late and already having pregamed, wants to know why I didn't take him along for the ride. And Nico Dawson, having heard from the other two that I probably bought a one-way ticket to some destination across the planet, wants to know if he should watch my apartment for break-ins.

These guys.

Next: take out all the garbage. Pay the rent and the bills. Go through the fridge and throw away anything that's on the verge of spoiling. Take out the garbage again. I don't know how long I'll be in Michigan. I don't know how long it will take to get answers from Cindy, and even if I don't, there's still Dad's hometown to check again. There might be something I missed. And if I could just *understand*....

I'm in a cab on the way to trivia night when the alert comes in on my phone.

It's the kind of pop-up message I'd usually ignore, but this one is from the app that I use to book all my flights.

And mine has been moved up...by ninety minutes.

I curse under my breath, drawing a glance from the cab driver. I should tell him to turn the car around right now. I don't have time to go to a trivia night. But Eva's expecting me to be there, and I'm not some fucking coward who's going to bail on her via text message.

The traffic is heavy for Saturday night, and when the guy pulls up at the curb, I'm ready to tear the door off and burst out onto the sidewalk like the Hulk. Instead, I shove a twenty into his hand. "Stay here. Five minutes. I'll be back out. Okay?"

He throws his hands up like I've made an impossible request. "All right. Five minutes."

The trivia night is at a different bar—a fancier one—and the main floor is crowded. The trivia itself, judging by the signage, is on the second floor and I take the stairs two at a time.

Our crowd is easy to spot.

There's Ash, laughing over beers with Gunnar and Nico. Day and Wes stand together off to the side, and huddled next to them, almost in the shadow of the corner, is Eva.

She's deep in conversation with Whitney, who reaches out and pats her shoulder in what I can only assume is meant to be reassuring, but Whitney is a little overenthusiastic. I weave my way through the tables toward them, coming up just in time to hear Whitney say, "—tell him how you feel. There's only one way to get over this, and that's by going through." She pauses for a dramatic breath. "Some of the great hardships of our lives are not meant to be avoided, but rather faced head on, so that—"

"Hey." I come up behind Whitney, trying to ignore the sensation of my stomach sinking right into my shoes.

Whitney turns, her eyebrows rising. "The man of the hour. I'll get out of your way." Her eyes flick back and forth between me and Eva. "Best wishes to you both," she says finally, then goes to stand next to Wes, who curls his arm protectively around her. I can feel Whit's eyes on us.

And then I feel nothing at all, except Eva's wide, green gaze. "Ben," she says softly.

"Listen." The words tumble out one after the other, like pearls on a string. "I can't stay. I know I said we'd talk, but I have a flight to catch."

"What?"

"I'm going to Michigan. They might have answers. Answers about my dad. Answers about where he came from, and why he pushed me into a career he hated. I have to know." My blood is on fire. "I have to know why he did that. Because it meant that I was in that Humvee when the bomb went off. And that—shit, *that* —that changed everything for me. And I know you've got your own stuff going on—"

"You don't know."

"I know you're scared, Eva. And I know you needed someone to get you writing again. And I'll always... fuck, I'll always treasure that week we spent. But you don't have to pretend you want that forever. Not for my sake. We don't have to live a lie."

I take her face in my hands and kiss her. As deeply as I can. As quickly as I can. Because that cab is waiting, and if I stay here much longer, my heart will shatter. And if it does—if a bomb goes off underneath my feet one more time—I'll never be able to stop looking for the answers.

"I loved it," I tell her when I can finally pull away. "I loved every minute of it. And I'll let you know when I'm back in the city."

I turn and go before she can say the words that will destroy everything.

"Ben!"

My hand is on the door handle. The cab driver is waving me inside. I can't stop. I can't ever stop, otherwise—

"Ben, what the fuck?"

I turn around to find Whitney barreling across the sidewalk at me.

"What the *fuck*?" It's the shortest sentence I've heard her say. "Jesus, Ben, what are you thinking? What the hell is in Michigan that's so important you couldn't talk to Eva?"

"The answers. To all the shit with my dad. Why his family placed him up for adoption when he was a *teenager*. Why—"

Whitney snaps her fingers in front of my face. "Stop. Stop that right now. There are no answers in Michigan, Ben. There are only more questions."

"You can't know that." The cab driver is getting impatient.

"Oh, I can. I had a dad who died too. And there are *never* any answers that anybody else can give you. What you want is for him to explain himself, and that is *never* going to happen. It's not going to happen, Ben." She stabs a finger behind her at the bar. "Eva is waiting in there, looking as pale as I've ever seen her, because she thinks it's over between you two. Because she thinks that whatever some random woman in Michigan can tell you is more important than what she has to say. She's trying to *protect* you, Ben, and you're walking out. Don't fucking do it."

"I have a flight."

"You have a woman who loves you. And if you want answers, hers are the only ones that matter."

My heart pulses and aches, and as Whitney faces off with me, the urge to get on a plane, to *move*, to find, fades. In its place is a fiery need to see Eva.

I open the door to the backseat, grab my bag, and wave the cab driver off.

"Go back in," Whitney says.

I go.

25

EVA

I'M ALMOST to the exit.

Almost home free.

If I can get out of here, I can call a car. I can go back to my apartment. I can shut this whole ridiculous adventure out and pretend it never happened, pretend I never got so close to risking someone I love for something that doesn't matter at all.

I'm about to push the door open by the broad metal handle when it swings outward, and there he is.

"That was fucked up," Ben says.

"I killed my entire family."

He stares at me.

That's not how I wanted it to come out. That's not how I wanted this conversation to go. But I've been holding it inside for twenty years, and I can't stand it anymore. Not when I feel this way about him. Not when all I want is to wrap my arms around his waist and press my cheek into his chest and let the rest of the world fall away.

Another heartbeat goes by, and another.

"Okay." He runs a hand through his hair. "Whitney was right."

All my defenses instantly snap into place. "Did she tell you?"

"She told me it was more important to talk to you than get on a plane to Michigan. She was right."

"I can't be with you."

Ben shakes his head. "Again with the whiplash."

"I'm as good as a murderer."

He holds out his hand and I take it. "Why don't we go somewhere else to talk about this?"

"No." If I go somewhere else, I'll have swallowed all these words, all these horrible truths, and I will never say them. Not ever. I have never said them aloud to another person, and even a two-minute walk down the sidewalk will keep me from saying it to Ben. "If I'm going to tell you, I'm going to tell you right now."

His eyes are steady. There's no flare of hate, no suspicion. He's looking at me like he loves me. And that's almost enough to break me.

But not quite.

I stand up straight and take a deep breath.

"When I was nine, my older sister Emily—she was perfect." My throat is tight and painful, and it takes everything I have to get these words out. "She was kind of a prodigy. Advanced beyond her years in everything, and my parents... they wanted to make the most of it. So I...fell by the wayside a little bit."

"They left you alone?"

"They left me with a nanny, Lola, who came with me to all my school events. You have to understand; Emily just needed...*more*. More than school could give her. So my parents gave her everything they could. Extra classes, almost every night of the week. Seminars at the local college on Saturdays. Now, I think they were trying to stay a step ahead of her, but it was hard. In comparison, I must have seemed like an idiot."

"I'm sure they never thought that," Ben says, and those eyes are filled with compassion. "There's no way they did, Eva."

"They thought I was...slower. They thought I'd never catch up to her. I heard her at the bonfire. Let me get this out."

"Okay." Ben holds my hand. He doesn't let go.

"I was taking ballet lessons that year." The memory comes back to me as strongly as if I'm still in that studio. I would have done anything to be the best in my class. I danced until my feet were so sore I could hardly walk. I wanted to catch up with Emily. I tried so hard. "And in the spring, we were supposed to have this recital."

It had been so close to winter that not all the snow had melted yet. I was cold in my little tutu and leotard, standing there with Lola outside the studio, waiting for them to show up.

"The morning of the recital, my parents told me they couldn't make it after all. Some visiting professor had offered to meet with Emily, and they only had time to make it to one thing. They chose Emily, again, and I lost it." I can still remember the heat in my cheeks and how raw my throat got from shouting at them. "I screamed and cried and begged for them to come to the recital. They were running late, and my mother was irritated, and she gave my dad this look."

I'll always remember that look.

"And he looked back at her, like—*what else can we do?* And he shrugged his shoulders, and then he said, 'Don't worry about it, Eva. We'll cut the meeting short and come see you at your recital.' I could still feel how off things were when they kissed me goodbye and left me with Lola."

"You were *nine.*"

"It didn't matter." My chin is starting to quiver. "It never mattered after that, because while they were on the way to my recital, a truck driver fell asleep at the wheel, crossed the centerline, and crushed their car."

Ben's hands fly to my shoulders, bracing me.

"It was instant, I guess. But the thing is, Ben, you learn from that. And I can't... I can't risk you the same way."

He folds me into his arms then, not saying a single word, and I break.

Twenty years of pent-up emotion pour out of the wounds in my soul, and I soak his shirt with my tears, trying to stifle the sobs with a knuckle in my mouth. It's a relief. It's mortifying. It goes on and on and on, until finally I gasp in one full breath, and then another. And then, at last, I step away from Ben and wipe my eyes with my sleeves.

"No wonder you didn't tell anyone you needed help with your book."

"I'm sorry." I'm a snotty mess. "I should have told you right away."

He laughs.

He actually *laughs*, and the sound is a balm to my soul. "Yeah? That's how you wanted to open things on the first date?"

"I should have been honest with you."

Ben cups my face in his hand and lifts my chin. "You were."

"I love you and I'm afraid that if I need you too much, you'll die."

"I love you. And that's ridiculous. You didn't kill anyone. And even if you needed me that much...." He shakes his head. "If I died doing something for you, I'd die a happy man," he says gently, and then he kisses me. And it's so possessive and soft and searching and deep that it finally cracks the frozen shards in my heart, destroying the stupidly complex gate there and melting it down until I am nothing but an open soul to him. His touch is rain in the desert. His kiss is light in the dark. And I never want to live without it again.

When I come up for air, I take a breath of the sweet possibility of a new life and give Ben a businesslike nod. "That's what I wanted to tell you. You can go to Michigan now. Get all the answers you need, and then come back, okay? I don't want to spend too many nights without you. Not to be needy."

He looks down at me, a smile spreading across his face. God, it's good to see it. It's more than good. It's the best thing I've ever seen in my life. "I have all the answers I need, right here."

"But what about your dad?" I protest. "That's *weird*, to be on someone's family tree and then switch families at such a late age. Don't you want to find out?"

"Are you asking me for another writer's retreat? Because I swear to God, Eva, I'm not getting on another plane unless you're coming with me."

"I don't get carsick on planes," I tell him.

Ben pulls me out onto the sidewalk, into the summer air. The night seems weighted with hope. "Then we'll fly. Forever, if you want."

"First class?" I joke.

"Coach," he says, deadly serious. "But I'll treat you like a queen."

"You have yourself a deal."

EPILOGUE

"No."

I stand in the doorway to Eva's office with a big grin painting itself across my face. "I didn't say anything."

"You didn't have to say anything. I can hear you breathing. You're so *loud*."

This is one of my favorite things about Eva Lipton. She gets so cranky when she's on a deadline. She was on an especially tight one after we flew to Michigan, last-minute, to discover that not only had my father's dad been a complete asshole, he was also not my father's... original father.

It was a mess.

And Eva had been right. There were no answers there.

I'll never know why he wanted me to join the Army. But what I *do* know is that he'd want me to be with Eva.

"I crept here as silently as I could."

She lets her head fall onto the back of her chair with a groan. "It's not right, you know. The way you do this to me."

I'll admit it; it's for me as much as it's for her. I've spent most of the last year getting my own private investigator business off the ground. Eva's right. It makes more sense to get paid for all my travels. Plus, I can almost always take her with me when I go abroad. Tax write-off!

"Sweetheart. My dearest." I go into the room and spin her office chair away from the sun-soaked desk so the rays catch in the tangled mess of her hair. This is Deadline Eva with a capital D. She needs the final chapters sent to her editor in three days. I press her legs apart with my hands and kneel between her knees. "I would never do anything to you that you didn't want."

"I want to finish my book." That's what she says with her words, but with her hands on the side of my face, she's saying something else entirely.

"And I want you to finish that book too. I also want to tell you news about Ash. But I guess that can wait."

She leans forward as if she can't resist the pull and kisses me. I can taste the little noise she makes in the back of her throat. It's somewhere between relief and irritation, and it always means she wants me here. It doesn't matter that we've lived together for a year now. The taste of her will never be anything less than a new continent to explore, and I put my hand around the back of her neck and find my way around her tongue and teeth until she pulls back, gasping.

"I don't have any *time*. You can't come in here and—"

"How are your shoulders?"

Eva makes a face and leans back in her seat, one hand going up to rub at the curve where her neck meets her shoulder. Then she sticks her tongue out at me. "That's not fair."

"It's *more* than fair to be observant."

"Can't you observe something else while I finish my book?" Her expression is stern for a fleeting moment, and then she loses control. "Can't you ever just let me suffer in peace?"

"No. But I'll let you suffer in company."

"That doesn't sound much better, but—oh!"

It still surprises her, my prowess when it comes to removing her panties. A quick hook of my thumbs and a tug, enough force to win the brief battle against her office chair, and I toss them backward into the bookshelf that holds copies of all her published titles, paperbacks, hardcovers, and special editions all.

"Those panties are decorating my bestseller covers," she says as I push her dress up to her waist and tug her down to the edge of the chair. "How dare you, Ben? Always waltzing in here and...." Her words cut off in a low groan, because I have licked her at her wet, molten center, just the way she likes. And if there's one thing I know about Eva, it's that nothing relaxes her like oral sex.

She opens her legs wider as I tease her, her head falling heavily back on the chair again and her hips rocking upward into my face so hard I have to hold her hips in place with both hands.

"No, don't—don't do that—come on, Ben. Don't tease."

It's such beautiful begging, and her deadline is so close that I relent.

And give her what she really wants.

Which is my mouth where it counts, the little nub of nerves at the top of her opening that turns her into a wild animal.

I press my lips over it, sucking her in, and Eva's fingers turn into claws on the arms of the chair. No flicks of the tongue, no fucking around for her—just a steady suction and the broad, flat surface of my tongue against her. Pulsing like the beat of her heart. Not too gentle, not too rough.

I feel her orgasm coming like an earthquake. The trembling starts down low, somewhere at the outside of her hips, and tunnels inward until she cries out *"Ben, I'm coming!"* and I know she is, because I'm lapping up the sweet taste of her like I'll never get another chance.

You never know.

Eva's fingers wind through my hair as I bring her down from the high, pressing sweet kisses to her unbelievably soft skin until the moment she puts her hands on my face and pulls me upward.

"You. Cannot. *Do.* That." She's trying her best to be firm, and her effort sparks a warm glow somewhere in the middle of everything else.

"But I must." In a burst of chivalry, I wipe my mouth

on my sleeve before I rise up on my knees to kiss her. "How's your shoulder now?"

"I don't know. My entire body is buzzing, thanks to you."

"You're welcome."

Eva shakes her head, eyes bright, and leans down to kiss me again. This time, she bites at my lower lip then pulls away with a little shiver.

I could have her over this desk in an instant.

But that's not what I came here for.

"Go away," she commands, turning back to the computer. "I have work."

I stop the movement of the chair with one hand and turn her back. "First of all, there's no way you can work with your dress like that."

"I was waiting until you left to fix it, but if you insist." She shoves back from the desk and stands up, smoothing down the dress in a way that makes me jealous of the fabric.

"Second of all, there's something I wanted to ask you." I pull the box from my pocket.

"What?" Eva does see. She's caught sight of something on the hem of her dress and is busy picking at it. "I thought we already talked about dinner. If you want me to make something, it'll have to be takeout, because I—"

"Eva."

She steps forward with a little shriek. "What is *that*? Ben! You can't—"

"I can do whatever the hell I want," I tell her. "And what I want is to spend the rest of my life making dinner for you when you're on a deadline. And taking you on a trip to a little cabin by the lake as soon as you're done writing. And stripping you down, and laying you against pristine sheets, and making those sheets an absolute wreck by the time—"

"Yes! Oh my God, yes." Eva covers her mouth with her hands.

"Marry me, Eva." I finally get the words in edgewise and it makes her laugh. She kneels down to hug me and falls at the last moment, taking us both over onto the carpet with a muffled *thud*.

"I love you," she says, her voice like bottled laughter. "I mean it."

"I love *you*." I lean over and kiss my soon-to-be-wife chastely on the forehead. "Now get back to work."

For more books by Amelia Wilde, visit her online at
www.awilderomance.com

Made in United States
North Haven, CT
26 March 2022

17573862R00163